DUNGEON QUEEN

KARPOV KINRADE
LIV CHATHAM

http://KarpovKinrade.com

~ ~ ~ ~ ~

Published by Daring Books

~ ~ ~ ~ ~

First Edition
ISBN: 978-1-939559-65-4

~ ~ ~ ~ ~

Disclaimer

For Lux & Dmytry, for proving old dogs can learn a shit ton of new tricks. ~ Liv
And for all the Greek Mythology fans who want some sexy god love. Enjoy!

"WHAT YOU LEAVE BEHIND IS NOT what is engraved in stone monuments, but what is woven into the lives of others." ~ Pericles

Red eyes glowing in the crisp fall night.
Terror pulsing through my veins.
My breath comes in short gasps
as panic clutches my gut.
And then...the screams.

I WAKE WITH A START, MY HEART BEATING WITH such force I fear my ribs will crack. A sheen of sweat soaks my clothes, making my skin itch, and my head feels crushed in a vice. My eyelids peel open, but the light is too bright, and I squeeze them shut against the glare. Every part of my body aches, and a dread I can't define has me in its grip.

A nightmare. I must have been having a nightmare...but why do I feel as if I've been hit by a truck?

Through my anxious haze, music floats to me as if in a dream. Something stringed— a harp, perhaps— plays a calming melody that dances in my mind. I try to move, to sit up, to see where the music is coming from, but my body feels tethered to some dark place, and I moan, finally giving up, still keeping my eyes tightly shut.

The music pauses.

"Easy now," a deep voice soothes. "You will feel a bit discombobulated for a time. That's perfectly normal."

My pulse quickens. Someone's in my room. Someone definitely not my roommate, who 1: isn't a dude, and 2: would never use the word 'discombobulated,' and 3: doesn't have an unusual accent. Mediterranean, maybe?

I force my eyes open once again, blinking rapidly to ease the strain of the bright golden light saturating the room. Our dorm only has one tiny window that's directly in front of a tree, and the only source of light we have is a half-busted bulb so old it makes the space feel like a cave most of the time.

So where is this blinding brightness coming from?

I peek through my eyelashes as my vision gradually focuses.

Standing over me, I see a beautiful man. His short golden hair curls around a face so chiseled he could be carved of marble. Thick lashes frame his large, blue eyes and his lips are full, sensuous. But his attire is distinctly odd. A white tunic made from obviously expensive fabric stretches across his defined chest, and over his broad, muscled shoulders he wears a luxurious gold cape with matching trim around the hem. A gold sash, gauntlets, and an oak leaf headpiece— that I'd swear is made of real gold—accent his attire.

This is no cheap Halloween costume, and we're still a few months from that holiday, anyway.

I blink once, then twice. "Who... who are you?" My voice sounds strange, unfamiliar.

The man leans down and slides a bare arm behind my back, his muscles flexing as he helps me sit.

The room spins, and I clutch my head to ease my dizziness. "Am I sick?"

He sits in a chair next to my bed and presents me with a golden, emerald encrusted goblet. "Drink," he says. "You have been through an ordeal."

I have so many questions, but my thirst stills them all. I accept the ornate cup and take a test sip. The amber liquid is sweet with hints of honey and cinnamon, so I drink more deeply, delighting in the flavors playing over my tongue. When I drain the cup, he lifts a matching pitcher from the side table and refills it. By the time I've emptied the goblet a second time, my head is clearer, and my vision sharpens.

I look around. I'm definitely not in my dorm room. I'm propped on a canopied bed made of olive wood, and on each post, deep green vines crawl with glowing crystals that hang where flowers might normally bloom. The walls are painted with intricate murals of fae dancing under moonlight, the forests glittering with magic. At one side, a fireplace blazes with warmth, and on a stand nearby rests an ancient lyre with tortoise shell adorning its silver inlaid cross bar. Was that the source of the music?

"Where am I?" I ask the beautiful man.

"What do you remember, Lily?"

My eyebrows shoot up. "How do you know my name?"

"I know much about you," he says, his carved lips curving into a secret smile. "But first, it is important you remember what brought you here. I've found, over time, it makes the transition much more seamless if you arrive at the answers on your own."

What do I remember? I search my mind, but my memories are out of focus shadows I can't quite grasp. My pulse races and my breath hitches, but the man puts a hand on mine that both soothes me and ignites a spark of electricity between us, all at once.

"Breathe slowly." His voice is calm and comforting. "Temporary memory loss is perfectly normal. It will come back."

"Perfectly normal for what?" I search his face for answers, but none present themselves.

"What can you recall of yourself?" he asks instead.

I close my eyes and inhale, breathing in through my nose and out through my mouth. And as I relax, I scan my thoughts for clues of my arrival in this strange place.

MY NAME. I STILL KNOW THAT AT LEAST. My name is Lily Lemon, and my life has always come in threes. I remember my sisters first. I was born the third of three girls to a middle-class family whose only remarkable quality lay in how exceptionally unremarkable we actually were. We even looked alike, dark hair, green eyes with the same dusting of freckles over the same pert nose and lips a shade too wide. As the most academically driven of the three of us, I graduated high school in three years, then spent the following three years working three jobs to save up for college.

I was headed out of state. Out of town. Much like my father. When I was six, I followed him outside one morning, the pavement cold on my bare feet, the exhaust-fumes and cigarette smoke at my throat. He spared me one glance, hopped into his Dodge Viper and drove away. He never looked back. Neither did we. My mom remarried three years later, to a wonderful man we call Dad, and my biological father became known as simply *Michael*, or *him*, or *sperm donor*.

While he'd been running away from something, I liked to imagine I was running *toward* something. In hindsight, I was naive. My eagerness for the world was driven by stories more than experience. Nourished by hundreds of books and movies, I had high hopes for university life. I'd develop everlasting friendships, acquire a reluctant—but devoted— mentor who would see my hidden genius and mold me into a work of intellectual art, and I'd come into my own as I mastered the subjects that spoke so deeply to my soul.

This was my frame of mind when my parents and sisters loaded into our mini-van and drove me across three states to Bard University.

Along the way, we played silly road-trip games, just as we had when we were children, and when we stopped for the night at the cheapest motel we could find, my sisters and I squeezed together into a bed too-small with me sandwiched in the middle.

Sarah—the mischievous middle child—held one hand and Melanie—the most beautiful of us—held the other. We were each born a year apart, and though I was the youngest, I was the first to leave home for college.

"It's not going to be the same without you, Lil." Sarah's voice wavered in the darkness.

"I'll be back for Thanksgiving," I promised, my own throat tightening.

Melanie squeezed my hand. "You're going to do great things," she said. "Museums around the globe will fight over you after you get all your degrees."

"Or you'll travel and collect stories and become a world-famous anthropologist," said Sarah, who fancied traveling above all else.

"Or I'll end up teaching community college while

struggling to pay basic expenses," I said, voicing my greatest fear. "No one touts Classical Studies as a must-have career path."

"Nonsense." Melanie snorted. "There will be plenty of great jobs open to you. You could be a professor, a lawyer, a museum researcher… "

"I definitely do *not* want to be a lawyer." I rolled my eyes.

"But you're so good at arguing," Sarah said with a giggle. "Mom and Dad think you'd be *great* at that."

I nudged her with my shoulder but smiled, nonetheless. The fact that I tended to win the debates in our house no doubt had a part in why my parents were willing to sacrifice so much for my higher education. Out-of-state tuition wasn't cheap. But still, I didn't see law in my future. I'd always felt more drawn to the past. To myths and stories of old. To dead gods and even deader languages. Could I just get paid to study Greek Mythology? That would be the dream job.

"I'll miss you both so much," I said over the sounds of our dad's snoring filling the room.

When he snorted loudly and rolled over in bed, Sarah giggled. "At least you won't have to deal with that anymore. I'd give anything for a night of silence."

I didn't blame her. Every night, the terrifying snores of our father resonated throughout our small two-bedroom cottage. But I knew she was wrong. I'd miss even that.

The next day, my family joined me as I waited in the long registration lines, Sarah and Melanie taking turns pointing out every cute guy they saw. Then, they all helped carry boxes and suitcases up the three flights of stairs to my dorm room.

As I schlepped the last box through the long hall, soft music reached my ears, a tender melody played on a guitar. The Seikilos Song. The oldest known complete musical composition found engraved on a tombstone near Ephesus, an ancient Greek city. It was simple and elegant and—

My foot snagged on something, and I fell forward, spilling all my precious books onto the floor, smashing my wrist into the tile. The music stopped on a sharp, unharmonious chord.

"Are you okay? Let me help," called a smooth voice.

I looked up and into the eyes of a guy who could pass for a Greek god. He practically glowed with gorgeousness. His dark hair heightened his pale blue eyes, and the sexy smirk playing over his lips would have made my knees weak if I'd been standing.

A guitar hung from his back. It was a reddish-brown timber and straight-grained. Mahogany, like the one my sperm donor owned and would never let me play. The one he took with him, instead of me.

Before I could respond, the man knelt down to quickly repack my books, then tucked the box under one arm while offering his other hand to help me up.

At his touch, my skin tingled, and my cheeks flushed hot. "Uh, thanks."

"You on this floor?" he asked as I righted myself and reluctantly let go of his hand.

"Yeah, room 306."

His smile widened. "We're neighbors then. I'm 308. Let me walk you back." He winked as he added, "Wouldn't want you to trip again."

My faced burned with embarrassment, but I fell into step beside him until we reached my door. "I'm just there, if you need anything," he said, nodding his chin towards the room next to mine.

As he handed the box back, my door suddenly flew open to reveal Sarah, standing there and grinning. "Lil, I—" when she saw the boy next to me her eyes widened. "Hello, I didn't realize Lily brought a friend over."

"Oh, this isn't—"

But 308 beat me to it, holding out his hand to Sarah. "I'm Clay. Lily's neighbor."

Sarah blushed, her fair skin turning a pretty pink. "Sarah, Lily's sister."

"Well, Lily's sister, I'll let you get back to it then." He turned and bowed dramatically as he took my hand. "Lady Lily, we shall undoubtedly meet again soon."

Then he brought my hand to his lips and brushed a kiss against my skin. This time, my knees definitely did wobble.

He left, and my sisters pulled me inside, grilling me for the details on how I'd met the gorgeous Clay from Room 308.

After I told my short but definitely not sweet story, Sarah groaned. "Only *you* would meet the sexiest guy on campus by tripping over your own feet."

I wanted to argue, but she wasn't wrong. "Where are mom and dad?" I asked.

"They went to get you some snacks from the vending machine." She laughed. "Mom was worried you'd starve to death before the cafeteria opened up tonight."

They arrived a few moments later, and my mother looked around the room, sniffing in distaste.

I couldn't blame her.

The room itself was the size of a glorified shoebox, and to make matters worse, my roommate took up more than her share of space. Even though she couldn't have been here for more than a few hours longer than I had, she'd left her dirty clothes littering every square inch of the floor.

"This place is a mess," Sarah said, wrinkling her nose.

Melanie guffawed. "Says the Lemon who has yet to learn how to put away any of her own laundry."

Sarah shrugged. "I'm not *this* bad."

Actually, she was worse, but none of us had the heart to tell her that. She was a whirlwind disaster who always left a mess in her wake. Of the three Lemon ladies, Melanie was the tidiest, and as the oldest, was always picking up after us both. I fell somewhere in between, the dreamer who left piles of books in odd places, but otherwise, I generally kept my belongings neatly put away.

My mother, a tall woman with an aristocratic face that often looked harder than she meant it to, dabbed her eyes as I finished unpacking the last box. "So, this is it," she said.

"Just for now," I said, letting her wrap me into a hug. She towered over my 4'9" frame, but then, so did everyone in my family. I was definitely the shrimp.

"Oh, my little Lemon." My dad sighed, pulling me into a bear hug. With a paunch for a belly and beefy arms from his years hauling garbage as a sanitation worker, the combination made his hugs a little dangerous—but always wonderful. "Be good and work hard," he said, releasing me.

"I will, I swear it. I won't let you down." They'd put everything on the line to help pay for my education. I'd worked and gotten scholarships but still hadn't managed to cover everything. They didn't know I'd overheard them talking about getting a second mortgage on our house to cover the difference. It made my heart ache to think about the sacrifices they'd made for me.

Finally, it was time to say goodbye to my sisters. "Lemonade squeeze," Sarah said, recalling our childhood nickname for our group hugs. I embraced them tightly, the tears now flowing freely on all of our cheeks.

Melanie twirled her dark braid as she studied me. "Remember, Lily, when life gives you lemons…"

"Make lemonade of their heads," I finished. Another childhood saying we crafted in a fort one day. It didn't make a lot of sense on the surface, but for the three of us, it made all the sense in the world.

The moment they left, my world felt empty, and yet a new stirring rose in me, one of hope and excitement for what was to come.

2

"Everything flows, and nothing abides, everything gives way, and nothing stays fixed." ~ *Heraclitus*

My focus returns to the present, to the gorgeous golden-haired man sitting before me. There's a knock on the door, and the man leaves to cross the room and answer it.

He speaks softly to someone I can't see, then closes the door. He's carrying a platter of food when he returns.

My headache has faded, but my memories are still not complete. They come to me slowly, like a movie I'm reliving one scene at a time. I can't recall the specifics until the scenes play out before my mind's eye.

"Why won't you tell me what's happening?" I ask, shifting to stretch in the bed. As I sit up, my hair falls in loose waves around my face and down my back. How odd. I always sleep with it up in a bun, so it doesn't tangle in the night.

A sudden fear grips me, and I study my body for signs of injury. It's then I notice I'm not wearing my own clothes. I'm dressed in a white nightgown made of silk; the neckline beaded with seed pearls. My arms are bare, and despite the warmth of the fire, I shiver. The light sheen of sweat on my skin makes the thin fabric stick.

I swing my legs over the edge of the bed, straightening my spine. "I feel... strange," I say, testing the strength of my muscles.

"If I told you everything at once, it could send you into shock," the man says, setting the tray of food on the side table next to the bed. "Why don't you eat? You'll find it quite tasty."

On the platter is an array of mouth-watering food. Pastries baked with brown sugar, four different kinds of cheese, three types of crackers, figs drizzled in honey, strawberries floating in cream, soft boiled eggs with slices of avocado layered with olives on top, and miniature bagels with a strange purple spread.

Self-conscious about eating in front of a man I don't know and in a place I don't remember coming to, I nevertheless pluck a fig from the platter and study it.

"Did you know, every fig has the digested remains of a fig wasp in it?" I say as I pop it into my mouth, surprised at that random bit of knowledge still floating in my mind. My fingers are sticky from the honey, and I wipe them on a golden cloth napkin.

The man cocks his head, a small smile on his lips. "I did in fact know that, but I am surprised you do."

"I read a lot," I say as I continue to pick at the food until my hunger is somewhat satiated, wondering why fig wasps popped into my mind instead of more important memories I'd rather have. Seeing the food must have triggered a latent part of my brain, like looking at an old photograph.

"Where's my stuff?" I ask, hoping for something else familiar. "My phone?"

He smiles playfully. "You tell me, *Lilyitsa*," using a term of endearment for my name which I recognize as Greek from all the literature I've read. Face aglow in the hazy golden light, he sits, eyes closed, cradling the lyre in a lazy embrace while absently strumming the strings with an expertise born of talent, skill, and years of practice. Long, beautiful fingers pluck the chords, coaxing from them a melody that winds its way into my soul and curls up inside of me as if it's found a home.

My eyes drift closed once again, and memories resurface, pulling me into the story of the life I can barely remember.

I SPENT THE EVENING ALONE, REVIEWING MY notes for each class and reorganizing my books. By subject? By class? Or alphabetized? I couldn't decide.

My roommate never showed that night, but just before I headed to bed, I heard shouting coming from the hallway.

I opened my door and peeked out.

Clay stood in his door, legs spread wide, arms braced against the jambs to block a tall, handsome man from entering his room. He had the same dark hair as Clay, the same pale blue eyes. But his face was heavier, wider, filled out by age.

"Tell Father if he wants to berate me for my life choices, he can do it in person instead of sending my big brother!" Clay shouted, his brows drawn into an angry line and his face flushed.

The man sighed, straightening the cuff of his custom designed suit that just oozed money and power. "Clay, you and Father can't keep at this. The decision has been made. This summer you'll be interning at the firm and that's final." He gestured around him. "Unless you want to pay for all this yourself?"

Clay flinched. For a moment, the anger in his eyes turned to hurt. Then it was gone, cut away in a blink, a cold gaze left in its place.

The other man sighed, his tone softening. "Look, brother, it's for the best. Aren't you tired of fighting?"

Clay slammed the door in his brother's face. A muffled yell escaped from his room followed by the thud of knuckles on drywall.

The man snorted and turned, stiffening when he saw me. Then, with a shrug, stalked away.

I stood there for a moment, debating on whether or not to check to see if Clay was alright, or go to bed. I closed the door and returned to my room. I didn't know him well enough to insert myself into his personal business so boldly.

The next morning, I stood in my dorm hall

studying the map of the campus, my hands shaking in excitement, when I heard a familiar voice.

"And where are you headed, Lady Lily?"

I looked up and blushed at Clay who leaned against his door looking every bit as drool worthy as he had when I'd met him. With his backpack casually swung over his right shoulder and a devil-may-care expression on his handsome face, I nearly melted into a puddle of goo. It was almost impossible to imagine him as the same guy who'd slammed his door last night.

"I'm off to Greek Mythology," I said, holding up my schedule. "Professor Mandlin."

Clay smiled. "What luck, that's my first class of the day, as well. Shall we walk together?" He closed his door behind him, but not before I caught a glimpse of his mahogany guitar splayed out on the floor, steel strings ripped apart, the body caved in. He didn't seem to notice me looking, just bowed and offered his arm, adding, "I promise to catch you should you trip again."

I could see this would be a thing. I sighed, resigned to the fact my natural klutziness had already established itself as a known quantity of my personality. Oh well, it was bound to happen sooner or later.

We made our way across campus together as I

struggled to think of what to say. But since I'd never been great at ignoring the elephant in the room, I finally blurted, "Are you okay? I heard you arguing with your brother last night."

Clay's eyes shifted from me to his feet as he stuck his hands in his pockets. "Just a family thing. You know how it is. My father wants me to follow in his footsteps, but his shoes don't fit me as well as he'd hoped."

Actually, I had no idea what that was like. I was very different from my family—always had been—but they still encouraged me to be myself and follow my own dreams. "What are his footsteps?" I asked.

"Law," he said. "My family owns one of the biggest firms in the country. My brother is my dad's protégé and will inherit the whole thing, but I'm still expected to graduate law school and become a partner."

"What would you rather do?" I asked.

He shrugged. "I don't know, honestly. I've never been allowed to imagine anything else."

That broke my heart. "Is that why you're taking Greek Mythology? Are you using Classics as your undergrad to get into law school?"

He nodded. "It seemed the most interesting out of all my choices, which weren't many."

I sighed. "That's shitty. I'm lucky that I got to pick my major. I've been looking forward to this class for ages," I said.

"Why's that?" he asked.

"So many reasons." I grinned, unable to contain myself. "One, it's a required course for my major. And two, Professor Mandlin."

Clay raised an eyebrow. "Is he a big deal or something?"

"Just a world-renowned scholar with multiple bestselling books and articles everywhere."

"Oh no." Clay tilted his head to look at me, a playful smile on his lips. "Don't tell me you're one of those."

I walked a little straighter. "One of what?"

"The read-every-book-for-every-class-before-the-semester-even-starts kind."

I glanced up at him nervously. "It's overkill, I admit. But I love reading more than anything, and Greek Mythology is my favorite subject by far."

Clay's chuckle held a heavy melancholy. "You certainly seem passionate about the topic."

His sadness sobered me. "Maybe somewhere in all this you'll find your own passion, too."

"I certainly hope so, Lady Lily."

We reached the classroom and took seats by each

other as the rest of the students filed inside.

Professor Mandlin arrived last to loom large behind his desk like a god of his own making. He looked exactly as I imagined he would with thick, black, square glasses, a head of thinning gray hair standing on ends, and wearing a tweed jacket complete with leather elbow pads.

I sat, attentive, ready to learn from the master.

He began class with a story. I knew this by heart, of course, but I still reveled in the tenor of his voice as he brought the ancient myths to life.

"Zeus, the king of the Olympian gods, began his journey into that illustrious position with a prophecy, a bit of a self-fulfilling one, really," Professor Mandlin said, moving to lean casually against his desk. "It was Gaia, that first primordial deity born into the cosmos out of Chaos, who told her son, Cronus, that he would suffer the same fate as his father: to be overthrown by his own son. What would have happened if she hadn't told him?"

He paused and scanned the room, his brow arched.

We waited.

With a superior smile, Professor Mandlin nodded. "Well, it doesn't matter, because the fact that she did is the reason we're in this class today."

We all laughed softly.

The instant he opened his mouth to continue, we fell silent. "Unwilling to lose his Kingdom, Cronus swallowed each of his children whole to prevent them from taking his throne. Finally, his wife, Rhea, sought help from Gaia to protect her next child, Zeus, and when he was born, she tricked Cronus by giving him a rock—which he promptly swallowed."

He paused, stuffed his hands into his jacket pockets, and began to absently pace in front of his desk.

Again, we waited.

Finally, he tapped his finger on a book resting on his desk and continued, "Now, Rhea sent Zeus to Crete, and our sources differ in just who raised him. Some say Amaltheia, others Gaia. We'll study that in depth, later. In either case, when he came of age, Zeus left Crete to rescue his siblings, and rescue them he did, by giving Cronus an emetic which caused him to vomit his children."

Several of the girls in front of me wrinkled their noses. I ignored them and just listened with rapt attention. Greek mythology wasn't for the faint of heart.

"Of course, once they were freed, Zeus and his siblings were highly motivated to overthrow their father," the professor continued, resuming his strolling back and forth. It was clear he'd said these exact words many times before. He had his performance perfected. "Which they did in a vast war called the Titanomachy, and with the help of Hecatoncheires and the Cyclopes, Zeus and his siblings won. As for Cronus' fate after the Titanomachy? The Homeric texts, the Orphic poems, Virgil's Aeneid, and even the account of the Byzantine mythographer Tzetzes all differ. But in this, they agree." Again, he paused to look over the rows of students, scanning each row one by one, before adding in a tone of finality, "The prophecy was fulfilled. And after the defeat, Poseidon, Hades, and Zeus bickered over who would become king. They drew lots for the position, and..." He flashes that superior smile and shrugs. "The rest, they say, is history, or shall I say, Greek Mythology 101."

I laughed, along with everyone else. This was going to be such an awesome class.

"Parenting, it seems, has always been hard," he said with a friendly chuckle. "But never so challenging as for the Greek pantheon, which is fraught with stories of children overthrowing their parents. And some stories of parents eating their children, so I suppose it balances out."

A titter of soft laughter filled the room, which the

professor allowed before he posed the question I had been waiting my whole life to answer: "What is the purpose of embarking on this journey to understand the ancient mythologies of Greek history? What relevance can they possibly hold for us today? This is your first in-class assignment. Begin your essay now."

My heart raced in my chest as I pulled out a pen and paper and begin to write. I was filled with an eagerness neither subtle nor flattering, but I didn't care. The answer to this all-important question burned in me, and I needed to write it in a way that did justice to the truth. Everything I'd read coalesced in my brain, mutating and growing into a new kind of thoughtful expression. Like when my mother taught us to bake, taking disparate and separate ingredients: An egg, a bit of baking powder, oil, cocoa and somehow creating a delicious cake from it all.

The essays, the online lectures, the books I'd read, the original myths in various translations, I'd absorbed them all, adding each ingredient into the bowl that was my mind. I'd spent years mixing it together, and now, it baked with each word, each sentence, forming something new.

This essay would be the culmination of it all.

I was the first to finish, despite having filled five pages with small, neat cursive, and even going so far as to quote from passages I'd memorized. Of course, I cited my sources, but most of the essay was 100% original thought, and I'd never been so proud.

I placed my paper on the professor's desk, expecting he'd take the essays home to grade later. But I flushed hot when he immediately picked it up and began to read.

Clay raised a curious eyebrow my way when I took my seat, then dropped his head and continued writing as I fidgeted like mad, waiting in silence.

We had ten minutes left in class when the others began turning in their work. By then the professor finished reading mine and looked up as he pulled his glasses off his hawkish nose and wiped them mindlessly on a dingy handkerchief.

I couldn't read his face, and I was nearly certain my heart would stop beating as I sat there, waiting to see what he said.

"Lily Lemon? Who is Lily Lemon?"

Disappointment rolled through me that he didn't remember me, even though I'd made eye contact when I'd dropped off my paper. But never mind that. It was a large class, and surely, he had a lot more important things on his mind.

I raised my hand. "I'm Lily."

He stared at me a long moment as other students turned to gawk, as well.

"Where did you get this from?" the professor demanded.

I swallowed; my mouth suddenly dry. "What do you mean? I wrote it just now."

He stood, holding my essay, and walked closer to my desk. "This is rubbish," he said.

My heart dropped into my gut, and I feared I'd vomit right then and there. "It... wasn't good?" My voice was nearly a whisper.

"Good? *Good*?" He turned to stare down the other students in the class, as if inviting them to join in his incredulity. "It is one of the most poignant and powerful articulations of the importance of Greek Mythology in modern culture I have ever read."

My eyes widened as my mind wrapped itself around his words of praise, and something in my chest swelled as relief crashed over me. He liked it? Not only liked it, but praised it profusely? It was more than I could have hoped on my first day. Like a dream, really. "Thank you, Professor. You have no idea how much that means to me."

"You would *thank* me?" he asked, slamming the paper on my desk with a sharp slap. "How dare you traipse into my class and turn in this clearly plagiarized work in an attempt to pass it off as your own. What author did you steal this from? Who should really get the credit? Because it is clear to me no girl, and certainly no freshman, could have written this masterful essay."

All the relief and flattery I'd felt just a moment before melted suddenly into rage and indignation, like an erupting volcano. With all the power I possessed, I battled the tears burning my eyes. I stood, my notebook falling to the floor in a loud clank as I attempted to face-off the man before me, even though he was several feet taller than myself.

"How dare I?" I asked, finally finding my voice. "How dare *you*, sir. I have never, nor would I ever, plagiarize another's work. These are my own words unless otherwise indicated by the handy use of quotation marks." Someone in the back of the room snickered at that, but I ignored them. Heat burned through me as I glared at this professor who had entirely lost my admiration and respect in that very moment. "Your accusations are baseless and sexist. If this is plagiarized, prove it. Go to your computer and find the origin of these words if they're not mine."

He stared at me a moment longer, then stomped back to his desk. "Class dismissed. Read Chapters 1-3 and be prepared for a test on Wednesday."

I was shaking when I stormed into the hall, my vision blurring with the tears I could no longer hold back. I walked with my back straight and no real idea where I was going. I only slowed when I felt a hand brush my arm.

"Lady Lily," Clay said softly. "That was garbage what he just did. Don't worry, no one believes you plagiarized."

I stopped, turning to press my back against the wall as I let my long hair fall over my face, covering my tears. "I can't believe he would do that," I whispered, my hands still balled in fists around my notebooks.

Clay offered his arm and smiled, dimples creasing his perfect cheeks. "Allow me to buy the lady a coffee. Let's not let that prick ruin a perfectly gorgeous day." He grinned.

The butterflies in my stomach rose to chase my anger and humiliation away, and flushing, I nodded and slid my arm through his. The contact sent shivers of pleasure up my spine.

Maybe this day could still be salvaged, I thought as I walked side by side with the sexiest guy at school.

But I should have known better, my life always came in threes. My bad luck was just beginning.

3

"THE ONLY TRUE wisdom is in knowing you know nothing." ~Socrates

LOUD BELLS CLANG IN THE DISTANCE, PULLING me out of my memories once again. The beautiful man playing the lyre suddenly stops, his full, sensuous mouth pinched into a tight line. "We've run out of time, I'm afraid."

My heart leaps as he stands and holds out a hand to help me out of bed.

If Clay was sexy, this man is positively divine by comparison. He makes Clay look mediocre at best, and that's saying something.

"Does that mean you'll tell me what's going on

now, or at least your name?" I take his hand, a zing of pleasure thrumming through me as our skin touches.

The man's eyes widen as his fingers squeeze around mine. "You can continue your recollections as we walk. As for my name... " he pauses to study me with keen eyes. "You can call me Ladron, for now."

Ladron? I took enough Spanish in high school to recognize the word. "Thief? Should I be worried?"

He raises an eyebrow in surprise. "It depends on who you ask," he says with a smirk.

I slide off the bed, my feet sinking into the thick carpet, my legs wobbling but regaining their strength as I take a tentative step and then, another. I don't let go of Ladron's hand, just in case I need him, but I'm surprised at how strong I feel. No, more than strong. "Why do I feel so powerful?" I ask, as I flex various muscles and marvel at the fire burning in my veins.

"You will find that feeling growing in time," he says, and, as usual, not really answering my question at all.

Then he studies me, frowning as he sizes me up and down. "We don't have time to bathe you, but you definitely cannot show up to my father's looking like that."

My shoulders straighten in offense. "Excuse me?"

His eyes soften. "Forgive me. You are truly lovely,

a rare flower beyond words, Lily, but my father has very high standards. You'll see what I mean soon enough. No matter, I have just the solution." He takes a step back from me and grins.

I blink, confused, and then, it happens so fast. One moment, I'm standing in a sweaty nightgown and the next, I'm wearing a beautiful blood-red gown that falls to my feet in layers of chiffon and silk. Around the hem, waist, and neckline tiny diamonds sparkle. Gold earrings dangle from my ears and nearly brush my shoulders, matching the square gold linked chain choker around my neck. My hair is piled on my head in loose curls that flow down my back, and the musk that was emanating from me is replaced by a light floral scent.

I hardly have time to process all this when he pulls aside the sheer curtains leading out onto a patio. "This way."

I gasp at the view. It's spectacular, like I'm standing in a travel advertisement. The foreground is a stunning collection of terra-cotta potted lemon and olive trees adorned with oleanders and violets, but it's the background that takes my breath away.

How did I get to the Mediterranean? I've only seen that Cerulean blue water on the internet, but it's a brighter blue-on-steroids in person, and it sparkles like it's glistening with diamonds under the dazzling sun. I'm at the top of the hill with a cascade of blue-roofed, limewashed buildings spilling precariously down to a white sand beach. Ships with sails dot the horizon.

"This is *heaven*," I say in delight.

Ladron laughs like I've just told a joke, only I'm not in on it.

"This way," he says, before I can ask him what's so funny. With a slight bow he offers me his arm and guides me down the white staircase.

"Where are we going?" I ask as we step onto a cobblestone street. I steal a glance over my shoulder for a peek at the villa we just left. My mouth drops open. It's a palace, a sprawling network of Grecian columns and terraced gardens. This isn't a place I could ever afford to stay at on my budget. I frown, confusion growing as I wonder once again how I got here and what the lemons is going on.

"You need to remember more before we get to my father," he says as he leads me down the path and through town.

"Care to help me along with a few hints?" I ask, though I become quickly distracted and slightly unnerved by the scene bustling around me.

Everyone is draped in simple, free-flowing tunics,

the men to their knees, and the women to their ankles. There's not a pair of jeans or a T-shirt in sight. And we're clearly walking down a market street. The stalls are made of wood and covered with braided leaves. They're selling ropes of garlic, clay bowls of olives in brine, and fresh caught fish. It's when I see a group of barefoot children herding a white cow with a stick that I stop in my tracks.

Something nags at the corner of my mind, and I turn, my eyes drawn again to the bright blue water of the harbor below. It's the ships I noticed before.

They aren't your average sailboats. They're triremes, the ancient Greek warships with three rows of oars and two sets of billowing sails.

"Where am I?" I look up at Ladron. "Is this some kind of movie set?"

A gust of wind ruffles his blond hair as the corner of his lip quirks in a teasing smile. "You're in heaven," he says.

I scowl at him. The only question he's answered so far, and he just threw my own words back at me. "Seriously," I insist. "What's going on here?"

He squints at the sun. "We must keep moving," he says. "We have a way to go yet."

He turns to continue, but I make up my mind I'm not taking another step until he gives me some real answers. As I watch him walk away, I can't help but notice the breadth of his shoulders and the sinewy play of his muscled thighs beneath his tunic. He matches this place in every way. He's beyond beautiful, hot as sin, and enticingly exotic.

He glances back at me and raises a questioning brow.

"I'm not going anywhere with you until you give me some answers," I say, folding my arms.

Everything about this place is off. This shouldn't be possible, any of it. Nothing makes sense, and a cold dread is growing inside me. My heart begins to race, and I know in my gut something is wrong. Really wrong.

Sweat beads on my forehead and a wave of nausea washes over me.

Ladron returns to my side, bracing my elbow to help steady me. "I know this is confusing, and if telling you everything would make this easier, I would. But it won't." He looks around, then nods his head at a nearby stall that's selling a variety of grapes, figs, oranges and other fruit.

"How about a refreshing elixir to help clear your mind?"

Before I can reply, he ushers me to the stand and asks for some lemonade.

I watch, dazed, as a young woman with dark eyes squeezes the lemons, adding water and honey. She hands me a silver goblet and I gulp the cold beverage down, desperate to quench my dry throat.

"Well done," Ladron says softly. "Now let your mind relax and see what you can recall."

Cup clenched in my hand, the metal cool against my fevered flesh, I close my eyes and dive back into the past.

BEING ACCUSED OF PLAGIARISM WASN'T HOW I expected to start my academic career, but I tried not to let it ruin everything else. The next few days flew by. I rarely saw my roommate, who introduced herself as Sam and didn't seem inclined to actually attend classes, only parties. But I saw Clay quite often. We had dinner together that first night, then breakfast the next morning. And thereafter, each day, he bought me coffee, sweetened with honey and cream, just the way I liked it, and the warm gooey feeling I had in my stomach whenever he walked by only grew.

I Skyped my sisters each night, sharing every detail of my life at college. They were outraged on my behalf at Professor Mandlin. Sarah offered to make lemonade of his head, and Melanie whispered a few choice swear words about his anatomy.

But I was determined to change his mind about me, and by Wednesday I was ready to own my first test in Greek Mythology, misogyny be damned.

Clay sat behind me, and when Professor Mandlin arrived, wearing the same tweed jacket, his scowling gaze swept the room until it landed on my face.

I scooted down and tried to make myself smaller in my chair. So, he hadn't forgotten a thing. That sucked lemons. I needed a fresh start.

There was no preamble. The professor just passed out the tests and sat down at his desk, glaring at us. "Begin," he said.

So I did. It was half multiple choice, half essay, and I soared through it as if propelled by Icarus's wings. Once again, I finished first, but this time I waited until a few other students turned their tests in before I slipped mine onto his desk. I crept back to my seat as invisibly as I could.

We were promised our grades on Friday, and my stomach felt tied in knots as we left. "How did the lady fare?" Clay asked, catching up to me in the hall.

"Objectively, I would be surprised if I missed any of the multiple choice," I mused, analyzing aloud. "The essays are more subjective, though. He could be a real dick there if he wanted, so I guess we'll see." Then, remembering I hadn't been the only one to take the test, I belatedly asked, "And you?"

He shrugged. "It is what it is. How about some pizza?"

I reached out and squeezed his hand. I hated seeing him so dispassionate. If only he could discover what he truly wanted to do with his life. No one should have to live someone else's dreams. "Pizza sounds great."

We left the building and headed across the lawn to a pizza truck parked near the library. It was hot and humid, the last gasps of summer as autumn would soon make its claim. I looked forward to the fall, with pumpkins and cooler weather.

"I envy you, Lady Lily," Clay suddenly said. "It's rough, being on Professor Mandlin's bad side. Especially when you're innocent."

"Yeah, did you catch that look he gave me?" I winced, picturing his scowling face in my mind.

"Couldn't miss it. If I were you, and I was accused of such crap, I don't think I would've walked back in that class." His voice took on an admiring edge. "You've got guts. How do you do it?"

I blushed a little at the compliment and shrugged. "I just make lemonade with their heads."

Surprise flashed over his face. "Say that again?"

I grinned sheepishly. Way to go, Lily. Now, he'll think you're some kind of axe murderer. "Just something my sisters and I came up with as kids," I mumbled. "It's our way of fighting back."

"A bit gruesome," he said, and then his eyes lit. "I like it."

We ate our pizza, and I spent the rest of the day in the library studying.

The next few days I fought the obsessive urge to logon to the website and check my grades every hour. I settled for once a day, in the morning, but every time I checked, my test remained ungraded. At first, I shrugged it off with ease. But as Friday neared, I felt on edge. I could sense when things were about to fall apart. It always felt a certain way. Like exhaust-fumes and cigarette smoke at my throat.

The day of class, when I heard other students talking about their results in the hall on the way to class, I grabbed my phone to check for my grade a final time. Nothing.

"Got your results yet?" Clay asked, falling into step beside me.

I frowned up at him. "No. Did you?"

He shook his head and held open the door.

The moment I stepped foot inside, my worries

were confirmed. One look at Professor Mandlin's face said it all.

"Lemon," he called out, his tone harsh as he stood behind his desk clutching two copies of the test in his balled-up fist. "Lemon and Clay. Approach."

My heart jumped to my throat. Why had only *I* gotten the last name treatment? What had happened?

A quick glance at Clay showed he was just as puzzled, and the background hum in the room dropped the instant we joined the professor at his desk. Everyone wanted to hear whatever drama was about to go down. Tea was currently being made, and everyone wanted a chance to spill it later.

Professor Mandlin spoke straight to the point. "This makes twice now, Lemon. I don't harbor cheaters in my classroom. You're out."

"Cheaters?" I gasped. What fresh hell was this?

He slapped the two tests onto his desk. Mine was on top and had a big red "F" circled on it. "I suppose you're going to claim that you're once again the sole author of this? Let me make it easy for you. Here's the evidence to the contrary," he said through clenched teeth as he pulled the bottom test out and presented it to me. "Did you really think I wouldn't notice?"

Whispers circled around the classroom as I squinted at the tests. There was mine, on the right. I glanced at the left, and when I saw the name, I could swear my heart quit beating.

Clay. Clay Davis.

I stared, confused, then took them both, scanning the multiple choice and then the essay portion. The tests were identical. Even the essays. Granted, a few words had been changed, but they were your basic synonyms, not concepts.

"I don't get it," I said. My voice, as soft as it was, rang through the still room like a bell—no, a foghorn. I glanced up at Clay, puzzled. "There's some kind of mistake here. Is this a joke?"

Professor Mandlin huffed a sarcastic laugh. "A joke? I assure you, no one in their right mind considers this class a matter of levity. The evidence is plain and simple. You copied off Mr. Davis for the chance at a stellar grade." His eyes shifted to Clay.

I waited, trying to calm my panic. Clay would make this right. He would explain that he'd been *behind* me. There's no way I could've even seen his paper to cheat.

But as Clay turned on me, I saw it in his eyes before his lips parted. "It's hard to believe this, Lily. I'm honestly hurt. Were you just pretending to be my friend in order to steal my work?"

There was a cold glint in his eyes as he put on his

performance. I couldn't believe it. I hadn't even seen it coming. I'd been played in the nastiest possible way.

Worse, no one would believe my side of the story.

I felt so cold inside, dead even. I couldn't even open my mouth.

"You insult this institution and this field of study," Professor Mandlin rasped. "Out. Now."

But he needn't have bothered giving that order. I was already running out the door.

4

"MISFORTUNE SHOWS those who are not really friends."
~Aristotle

"HE CHEATED. HE BETRAYED ME," I GASP, looking down at the silver goblet in my hands, the taste of lemonade and honey still on my lips. I set it on the wooden table as Ladron drops a coin into the owner's palm.

"Shall we walk again?" Ladron says. His blue eyes search my face for answers I still can't give him. It's clear he's waiting for me to say something more, but what?

I sigh, exasperated by all of this. "What am I missing?"

The bell tolls again, drowning out his reply—not that he would have answered me, anyway.

"We must walk a little faster," he says, taking my hand in his and tugging me down the street at a more clipped pace than before.

His warm, strong fingers gripping my hand make me lose track of myself. I'm lost in the pleasant sensations of being so close to him. His magnetism and attraction draw me into his spell, and it takes me a moment to snap my thoughts out of that trance. I'd vowed never to let a guy into my heart so easily again, hadn't I? I frown as something teases the edge of my memory.

"What is it?" Ladron asks immediately. "What have you recalled?"

I chase at the thought, but it's like trying to catch the wind. "Just that guys can't be trusted," I snort, but even as I say the words, I wonder why I did.

"Ah, such is love," he says, shrugging his shoulders and giving my hand a gentle squeeze.

"No, not love," I say with an assurance that surprises me. I may be foggy on the details, but this much I know. It was never love.

He quickens his pace, and I have to nearly jog to keep up. His legs are so long, eating up the road, and it takes two of my steps for every one of his.

We are headed up a steep hill, and I prepare myself for sore muscles and shortness of breath, but strangely, my legs don't burn. In fact, it's quite the opposite. They stretch, as if eager for more. Suddenly, I want to run.

And I do.

Releasing Ladron's hand, I take off, grinning back at him as I push my body as far as I can. I've never felt so strong, the powerful flexing of my thighs and calves taking me further and faster than I've ever run in my life. I must've gone the equivalent of several football fields before Ladron catches up with me, laughing.

"If you're going to run, *Lilyitsa*, then at least run in the right direction," he teases, catching my arm and turning me west, up a side road that stretches before us in a long, winding path.

Again, the spark of his touch makes butterflies dance in my stomach, but then that feeling sours as I remember how I just went through this, and it didn't end well. I just can't remember exactly why.

"We're close." Ladron points as we round a bend.

I stare in awe at the palace that rises before me, about the size of three football stadiums. The columns are magnificent, over fifty feet tall. The bases and capitals are overlaid with gold along with the olive-leaved cornices that crown the complex. Jasmine and wisteria fall in perfumed clusters along the walkway leading to a door so massive ten full-sized chariots could easily drive through. Stone reliefs and elaborate carvings grace the walls, depicting scenes of victorious battles and portraits of kings.

"We're so close," Ladron says.

I tear my eyes from the splendor spread before me to look up at him.

"You have to remember the rest before you meet my father." There's an urgency to his voice that wasn't there before, and I feel even more frustrated by my stubborn memories playing hide and seek with my conscious.

"Do you think I'm not trying?" I ask, my irritation boiling over. "I understand you have your reasons for not just telling me, but badgering me isn't going to make this go any faster. If I knew how to remember everything, I absolutely would. This isn't all that fun for me, you know."

He doesn't look annoyed, just amused. "Indeed," he murmurs, his eyes lighting in a way that makes my stomach somersault. His grin creases his cheek, making me want to trace the subtle lines with a fingertip. "Are you up for a detour?"

I frown. "I thought it was all rush, rush, rush to see your dad," I say.

"This will take but a moment," he replies, shrugging his broad shoulders. He steps onto a stone path, winding away to the left. "Dogs," he asks suddenly. "Do you like them?" He doesn't wait for my answer but disappears around a clump of small-flowered tamarisks.

He's so confident I'll follow. And I do, a little annoyed but getting used to him refusing to provide any clarity.

I nearly run into him. He's stopped just on the other side of the shrubs. He stands on a kind of balcony, overlooking a garden below where page boys are saddling horses with gold-tasseled blankets and silver-inlaid saddles.

"Dogs?" I ask as I join him at the marble railing. "Love them. But why?" Rather than answer, he merely nods his chin to the right.

A young boy has arrived, his thin arm struggling under the strain wrangling three tan Cretan Hounds —slender dogs with long curly tails and wedge-shaped heads.

The dogs begin to bark, ready for a hunt, and panic grips me, darkness clouding my vision as I fall to my knees.

I hear Ladron's voice calling my name as if from a distance, but I'm transported to my past once again.

I SAT IN THE DARK, HUDDLED ON MY BED UNDER a heart-shaped patchwork quilt my sisters made to remind me of home. I hadn't eaten or spoken since I left Mandlin's class. The thought of putting anything in my stomach made me want to vomit. All I could think about was the end of my dreams.

As far as cheating accusations went, the average, run-of-the-mill charge would get me suspended and jeopardize my financial aid, but an accusation from the esteemed Professor Mandlin held extra weight. I'd probably get expelled, with nothing to show for my college attempt but debt my parents would still be on the hook for.

My laptop chimed, alerting me to an incoming call from my sisters. I considered ignoring it, but they'd worry if I didn't answer.

Begrudgingly I crawled over my bed to my desk and pulled the computer to my lap.

When my sisters saw my face, they immediately stopped chattering to ask what had happened. After I explained, they erupted in rage.

"It's not fair," Sarah said.

I just sniveled in response; my nose so raw it burned.

"Sue them," Melanie ordered.

"What an ass," Sarah said, shaking her head. "I can't believe it."

"Sue him," Melanie said again, her jaw locked in anger.

"He seemed so nice," Sarah said, still shaking her head.

"Sue the professor," Melanie said again, her refrain on repeat.

I didn't have much to add to the conversation. Their support and love made more of a difference than anything else could.

But my heart hurt. Why would Clay do this? I'd thought we were friends... more than friends even. Or at least on the way to something more. We'd spent hours talking, dining together... and he brought me my morning coffee every day. Was it all just so he could cheat off me? How had I not seen his true colors?

"Really, they need a good lawsuit," Melanie was saying when I tuned back in. "Knock them all down a notch."

"*You* should be the lawyer," I said, my stuffed nose making me hard to understand.

"Don't just take this." Sarah leaned in closer to the camera, her eyes flashing. "Fight back. Don't let him get away with it, either of them. Clay, too."

I sat up.

"Make lemonade of their heads for reals this time, Lil." Melanie's evil grin framed in my computer screen made me laugh.

They were right. I wasn't going to win sniveling under a quilt. "I'll catch you later," I said, the anger inside simmering to a solid boil.

"Go get 'em," they said before the screen went black and I closed my laptop.

I swung my feet off the bed and marched over to Clay's door.

I'd make the lying bastard tell the truth, to me and to Professor Mandlin. I'd teach them both a lesson. Clay needed to learn that you don't just use people and toss them aside. And you don't cheat. Though how a college kid with lawyer parents hadn't learned that already was beyond me. And Professor Mandlin? He was going to get a swift kick in his khakis until he saw the light and stopped being a sexist, judgmental asshole.

I pounded on door 308 three times before it

swung open, revealing Clay's roommate Travis. His arm was possessively draped around a girl who looked glued to her phone.

"'Sup?" he asked, nuzzling her neck.

"Where's Clay?" I asked.

He squinted at my face, taking in the puffy eyes and the red-rimmed nose and hesitated. "Why? Thought you two broke up."

I snorted, letting the venom in my voice show. "None of your business why. And we were never together." Not because I hadn't wanted to be with him. I'd actually thought he was taking the time to get to know the real me.

"Okay, okay," he said quickly, holding up his hands like me meant no harm. "He's at Sigma Chi. Bahamas Night. They've got the sixty-foot water slide, kegs, the whole deal."

"Thanks," I mumbled.

I left and headed across campus to Greek Row.

It was late and long shadows spread over the path, dotted by the occasional flickering lamplight that provided only minimal illumination to the campus at night. I guess I'd spent longer than I thought talking to my sisters. I marched down the sidewalk, under the trees, listening to the crickets as I sorted my thoughts.

I had to play this cool if I wanted to win.

Should I act all innocent? Get him to confess while I recorded him on my phone? Was that admissible evidence without a warrant? Did those kinds of laws even apply to a student trying to clear their name?

Sigma Chi came into view, a brick Tudor style house with every window alight, kids partying both inside and out. I could hear the music as I cut across the grass, the bass so loud that I could feel it vibrate through me. The smell of weed and alcohol hung in the air. When I arrived at the door, I had to shout in single syllables for anyone to understand. "Clay? Clay Dav-is?"

Heads shook in confusion.

Finally, a freckle-faced guy pointed up the stairs.

I pushed my way up, through drunk frat boys holding red solo cups and finally arrived at the room above.

I found him at a pool table, wearing a straw hat and swim trunks. He held a cue stick in one hand and a beer in the other as a tipsy, giggling blonde draped herself over his shoulder. Her white t-shirt with the pink letters of Kappa Kappa Gamma stretched tight across her breasts looked like it was about to bust open, but he didn't seem to mind.

So, this was his real type. Melons over lemons. Figured.

Clay tensed the instant he saw me. To his credit, he didn't run. But then, I was a shrimp, hardly anything that inspired terror.

"Talk?" I shouted when I arrived to stand in front of him.

He drew his mouth into a line.

"What?" the blonde asked, looking to him and clamping a possessive hand on his chest that screamed 'this is mine.'

I felt like warning her to run away as fast as her tight booty shorts would let her, but it was far too complicated a conversation to have in this environment. Too many syllables.

With a nod toward the stairs, Clay handed her his pool stick. And after dropping a kiss on her lips, he pushed his way through the crowd.

We didn't speak until we stood across the street in the grass, next to Mangy Park, oak trees swaying above us. We wouldn't have been able to hear each other any closer to the cacophony of sounds. The boom of the bass reached us even here.

A young woman, about my age, nearly bumped into us as she passed. She wore a pink tank top and walked with a small grey cat on a leash. One of the oddest sights on campus yet.

"Why?" I asked, my voice hoarse from the crying and all the shouting in the fraternity house. "Did you need the grades that bad?" I was striving to be understanding. The better person. But shit, it was hard.

"Don't know what you're talking about, Lil," he replied, stuffing his hands in his pockets.

"Are you serious right now? You absolutely know what I'm talking about." His denial was stupefying. And since when had I become 'Lil?' Only my sisters called me Lil.

He sighed. "Look, I just came out here to tell you it's over. Leave me alone. That's it."

"Over?" I was astounded.

He took a step back toward the party.

"Hey, wait—" I began.

A growl from behind the trees interrupted me. It was low and deep, but loud enough we could hear it, even over the music blasting from the frat house.

"What's that?" Clay asked, jerking around.

I squinted, trying to see in the darkness.

Then, shadows sprang toward us.

Dogs. No. Monsters. They seemed to fly through the air, their jaws wide open, blue incandescent venom dripping from their teeth, razor sharp and ready to bite. Strangely, their eyes glowed, but not the white you usually see when light reflects off animal eyes at night.

These eyes glowed red.

Terror pulsed through my veins.

My breath came in short gasps as panic clutched my gut.

And then...the screams.

First from Clay, who couldn't look away from the dog's teeth, and stood immobilized in fear.

Then from the young woman turning the path toward us, the one walking her cat on a leash. She froze in place, her eyes going wide.

The unnatural hounds turned in tandem, their attention attracted by the pissed off feline hissing and extending its claws, body curled and ready to pounce. It pulled at its leash, but the woman clutched it, still too shocked to move.

I had only a moment to act, and my body responded on instinct, pushing me forward until I slammed into the woman and her pet, thrusting them out of the way of danger.

"Run," I shouted to her.

This snapped her out of her temporary paralysis, and she picked up her cat and ran away.

The dogs looked ready to follow, but I whistled to

catch their attention, which made Clay squeal and take a step back.

My heart pounded in my chest, trying to escape my ribs by any means necessary. Time seemed to slow as the villainous hounds trained their eyes back on me and growled, prowling forward in unison, like evil synchronized swimmers in dog suits.

I slowly backed up as I pulled my phone out to call 911. I just had to keep them calm long enough to get help.

As the operator answered, I felt Clay's hands on my back, shoving me forward, straight into the dogs' path.

I tripped and fell to my knees.

It was too late then. I could do nothing more than cover my face with my arms before the beasts were on me.

It was mercifully quick, and I dissociated from the pain.

Strangely, my last thought was wasted on Clay, wondering how it took me so long to see him as the despicable coward he was. He'd actually pushed me into the hounds to save his own sleezy hide. Go figure.

5

"WISE MEN SPEAK because they have something to say;
Fools because they have to say something." ~ Plato

I BLINK. WE'RE STILL STANDING ON THE
balcony, overlooking the page boys readying the
horses for the hunt.

"I died," I say, turning to look straight into
Ladron's eyes.

Relief suffuses his handsome face. "You did."

"So, I was right? This really is heaven?" Heaven
was Greece? Well, for me it was, but the average
person might expect something different.

"You've been brought to where you should have
been from the start," he explains. "Though it should

not have happened in that way. That night, with the hellhounds—"

"Wait," I interrupt. "You know about the dogs?"

"As I said, I know many things about you." His gorgeous blue eyes are slightly puzzled.

I follow the question with another. "And you know about 'making lemonade of their heads,' too, don't you?" He doesn't have to answer. I see it on his face. So. He hasn't really been ignoring my questions. He's been triggering my memories this entire time. The knowledge heals a part of me that Clay broke. "You'll tell me what's going on, now?"

His cheeks dimple with a smile. "My pleasure, Lily." He clears his throat. "You're a reincarnated goddess."

The word *goddess* short circuits my brain. He's acting so casual, like he meets reincarnated deities every day. But then, maybe he does. I swallow, trying to digest his words. "How can you tell?"

"Tell?" He asks.

"That I'm a goddess," I say.

His eyes light and a smile teases his lips. "You returned to the Mount, fully formed, as only gods and goddesses do. Though, as to which goddess you are, there's a bit of a debate. Normally, it's obvious, but your case is…rather unique."

"In what way?" I press, when he doesn't continue.

He glances back at the palace rising over us. "You'll see. Let's go, shall we? It's not wise to be late."

I follow him about three steps, and then it strikes me. I died. I really died. Tears sting my eyes. What must my family be going through right now?

"What is it?" Ladron asks, gently. He's back again, dropping a comforting hand on my shoulder.

The sympathy undoes me. "My sisters," I choke. My mom. My dad. They would have gotten a call that my body was found. They would have had to identify me, or whatever was left of my mutilated corpse. They'll have to plan a funeral and tell everyone what happened. Over and over they'll have to repeat the words, "My daughter is dead." "My sister is dead." And each time it will rip their hearts out a little more.

As I struggle to process that layer of sadness, another strikes even harder. I'm dead. Which means… I'll never see them again either. I've lost everything. My family, my life, my plans for the future. It's all gone.

I thought being accused of plagiarism and losing my standing at college was bad.

This is definitely worse.

I'm drawn into a comforting hug, but I only get about three good sobs in before another bell rings through the air. This one deeper and louder than the previous ones.

"Alas, I fear you must set aside your grief for now, *Lilyitsa*," Ladron murmurs into my hair. "We must hurry. It is time."

I peel myself from his hard chest. My heart is torn, but my pain is something I need to unpack in private, anyway, so I shove the emotions deep within me and put up a wall, hardening myself until I can be alone with my thoughts.

As he guides me around the shrubs to the original path, I wrestle my mind back to the present and to getting as much information as I can. "Why was I attacked by hellhounds? What were they doing on earth?"

He presses his lips into a hard line. "Hellhounds should not be able to penetrate the barrier between our world and yours. The truth is, I don't know why you were killed that night."

"So, are they still there?" I ask. "Just randomly killing people? There was another woman near me that night walking a cat. Did she get away safely?" Fear slices through me as I imagine hellhounds terrorizing humans, maybe even making their way to my family cottage. I shake my head, trying to dislodge the horrific image that settles into my mind.

Ladron shrugs, and I get the distinct impression he's leaving a lot out. "No, those particular hounds have been dealt with."

Our conversation is cut short as we join the steady stream of men and women entering through the palace's massive doors. The parade of velvet, chiffon, and satin glitters with precious stones and gold.

"Have all these people died?" I look to Ladron in wonder.

He chuckles. "No, Lily. It's not very often the divine return. These people are those Zeus has summoned to attend the celebration of assigning the kingdoms to the returning gods."

"It's the mother of all parties…" I begin, but my mouth turns dry. Had he just said… "Zeus?" I'm on…Mount Olympus?

He smiles wordlessly, and then we're through the massive doors and into the palace courtyard.

Music plays all around us, the sounds of harps and lyres mixing with the jingling of belly dancers. Hundreds of girls dressed in scarves, their arms covered with bangles. They're a swirl of color; red, purple, blue and gold.

"Who are they?" I ask, as Ladron takes my forearm and guides me forward.

"They're gifts for the gods that return," he says.

Gifts? People are just… given? Like slaves? That's a sour lemon to swallow, and the unease sits with me as Ladron stops before a gray-haired man swathed in purple. His eyes are so sharp, and his nose so pointed, he reminds me of a hawk.

"Her—" the man begins.

"Ladron, here," Ladron introduces himself. "With Lily Lemon."

The man knits his brows. "You're in the wrong palace, *Ladron*." He takes time to stress the name. "Hera has her—"

"There's no mistake," my escort insists. He points to the heavy, gold-trimmed scroll at the man's feet. "Just check, you'll see us there."

The man directs a skeptical gaze at Ladron, who lifts his chin and crosses his arms in a clear gesture that says, we aren't going anywhere until he checks his scroll. Finally, the stubborn man relents, and after a moment murmurs in perplexed surprise, "Interesting."

He stands aside and we pass, but I notice him giving me a strange look.

Before I get the chance to ask Ladron about that bizarre exchange, we're inside the palace, weaving through a maze of halls, all crowded with people in their finery, and then we enter the great throne room.

I suck in a breath and stare, trying to take in everything.

It really is a room fit for a god.

Shallow braziers hang from the ceilings and perch on floor stands, flooding the room with light. Each wall is adorned with battle scenes carved in stone and gilded with gold, silver, and precious gems, the light from the brazier fires making them sparkle.

A pool of water runs down the center of the room, starting ten feet from the entrance and ending before a mighty throne on a raised dais at the far end. On either side of the pool, couches are arranged, overflowing with velvet gold-tasseled cushions, some spilling onto the floor. A group of servants hover at the foot of each couch, holding platters of fruit, roasted meats, and engraved pitchers of wine, and behind them, belly dancers shimmy and shake, moving with ease, the rhinestones on their skirts clinking in beat to the rhythm of their hips. I can't help but notice that the number of dancers, servants and refreshments significantly diminish the further away a particular couch gets from the throne. There's a definite hierarchy here.

Ladron leads me to the last couch on the left. It's smaller than the rest and looks almost like an afterthought, boasting only two velvet cushions and one servant in attendance. And instead of girls at the back, there stands a single man, dark and mysterious, arms crossed with a bow slung over his shoulder.

He's so striking that it makes me do a doubletake. His bulging biceps catch my eye first. Then, the fact he's wearing leather leggings, laced up at the sides. Leggings? He's the first I've seen to wear anything but the standard issue Greek tunic. And he looks anything but Greek. His eyes are bright silver, and his dark hair is long and straight, clasped with oblong silver beads. Around his neck, he wears an open, silver collar choker with snakeheads on either end instead of clasps. The band draws my attention to his collarbone—or more specifically to his unbuttoned shirt that exposes the dip in his throat along with a firm outline of his chest. I catch a glimpse of a tattoo that looks like the body of a snake.

It suddenly feels a bit too hot in here. I consider fanning myself when I feel a flush burn my cheeks, but that just seems a little extra at the moment, and I'd rather not draw attention to myself.

Ladron follows my gaze—which is still fully locked on Mr. Tall, Dark and Sexy—and immediately tenses. "Mirk? Why are you here?"

Mirk tilts his head to one side and his silver eyes glitter. "What concern is that of yours?" he drawls in a mocking tone. His voice is like whiskey, smooth with a slow burn that only fans the flames of heat building in me. I could listen to him read even a grocery list without ever getting bored.

Ladron levels Mirk a look as he escorts me to the couch. "Sit, please," he murmurs before arching an expectant brow at the servant in attendance.

A gray-haired grizzled man obligingly steps forward with a slight limp. "A drink, my lady?" He holds up a terracotta jar of wine with knotted, arthritic hands.

I'm not much of a wine drinker—and if I'm being honest, even my whiskey drinking is pretty limited, but I nod anyway. As he fumbles with the cup, Ladron stalks behind the couch to draw Mirk aside.

I force myself not to turn around. I'm already attracted to Ladron, and if I'm honest, Mirk's got something just as sensual going on. So, I sit there, watching the servant try his best to pour the wine without slopping it on the floor. It's touch and go.

"Let me help," I say, rising to my feet.

He frowns and gives me a look that makes me feel like I've insulted him.

"Sorry," I say, sitting back down. "What's your name?"

That surprises him, like no one has asked him

that before. "Alfio, my lady," he says, offering me the wine.

"Thank you," I say.

I hold the cup and glance around.

Mirk and Ladron's voices grow louder.

I try not to eavesdrop, but that proves impossible as within ten seconds, Ladron and Mirk are nearly shouting as they cut each other off.

"I'll not have the likes of you hanging about—"

"You have no power here—"

"You're a fae, a capricious peacock of a—"

"Twiddling the strings of a lyre all day hardly makes you a master, you sack of wine—"

Their confrontation is drowned out as the belly dancers next to me begin jiggling louder, announcing the arrival of a redheaded youth at the couch next to mine. He smiles at me and then looks confused. After a few seconds, he leans over and whispers, "I say, you shouldn't sit there. I shan't tell. Hurry and get up."

"Why?" I ask.

He looks embarrassed—for me—as he whisper-shouts, "That's a god's couch. They've sent you to the wrong place."

A "god's" couch? I glance around, and sure enough, all the other couches now hold men. Really? Figures. The belly dancers all make sense now. I roll my eyes, and when I look back at my neighbor, he nods and smiles, like I'm about to admit I've made a mistake.

"Nope, I'm where I'm supposed to be." Ladron wouldn't make that kind of blunder.

My neighbor frowns doubtfully, but then, his wine and a few girls arrive at his side and he forgets all about me.

"Your wine, my lady," my elderly servant says, holding the goblet out to me. He's managed to fill it halfway.

I don't mind. I much prefer the light, refreshing zing of a lemonade.

The noise in the great hall falls silent just as Ladron shouts, "By Zeus, I'll not have Hades' son in her harem."

All eyes turn my way.

My cheeks burn as I turn to stare back at them. Did he just say harem? *My* harem? Weren't harems usually the domain of Arabic ruling-class men and such? Certainly they weren't expecting *me* to form a freaking harem? That's...insane.

But all thoughts of harems fall from my mind like autumn leaves when I see the figure lounging on the first couch at the head of the pool. The heat in my body turns to ice, and I choke, wincing hard as if I'd just sucked a sour lemon.

On the couch, surrounded by hordes of dancing women, with servants tripping over themselves to wait on him, is the one man I hoped death would spare me from ever seeing again.

Clay.

6

"MAKE the best use of what is in your power, and take the rest as it happens." ~Epictetus

A BELL RINGS AND SERVANTS PAUSE THEIR fawning to pay tribute as a herald makes an announcement.

"All hail Zeus, God of the Sky and King of all the gods," the herald says.

I reluctantly pull my eyes from Clay to watch as Zeus makes his entrance.

He's magnificent, curly gray beard, chiseled physique and all, but I can't concentrate on him despite the fact he's one of the most famous gods in history. I'm stuck on the fact that Clay—the rotten scoundrel who pushed me into the hellhounds to save his own skeezy hide—is *here,* and not only here, but sitting at Zeus' right hand. Judging by the sheer number of belly dancers crowded behind him, he's been given a position of great honor.

Clay freaking Davis. I can't even escape him in the afterlife. That's just rich.

As Zeus ascends the steps to his throne and raises his goblet, everyone follows suit.

"Welcome home," he thunders.

There's a bit of a hubbub after that, people laughing, clapping, and generally having a grand old time. Finally, Zeus lifts his hand again.

Everyone goes quiet.

"Let us begin." Zeus announces, his voice rolling deep across the room. "Rise and approach, Epimetheus. Welcome home. You have been sorely missed."

There's thunderous applause as Clay—the same cowardly Clay who squealed like a child—stands up, looking smug in a blue tunic trimmed with gold and sapphires.

I can only stare. But then, it makes sense, doesn't it? Clay as the reincarnation of Epimetheus? It explains the cheating on the test. The god of afterthought and excuses wasn't likely one to study.

But still, I can't say anything flattering about their standards of godhood if they accepted Clay into their ranks.

I sit there and try not to seethe. Finally, I tune into Zeus' speech only to hear, "And I will bestow upon you the lands north of the Cithaeron mountains, the kingdom of Hylica. Five hundred servants. One hundred virgins. Two thousand slaves…"

The list goes on and on. A few interesting items stand out, an "enchanted fishnet," and "the Helm of Terror." Not that Clay needs help in the inflicting-terror department. I wince, recalling my last glimpse of the hellhound's teeth.

"Kneel, Epimetheus," Zeus commands.

Clay kneels before the throne, as one of Zeus' cronies sticks a crown on his cowardly head. A real crown adorned with gold leaves and sapphires.

After the applause subsides, Clay returns to his couch, and my freckled neighbor looks my way, giving a low whistle. "Choice kingdom, that."

I don't reply, because I'm pretty speechless.

The couch resident on Zeus' left side is called, and the same scene plays out again and again. Eros. Thanatos. And more. Each receives a kingdom, servants, and a few magical items along with an allotment of virgins. Each one gets a crown.

But I notice a pattern. The further away from Zeus, the smaller the kingdom and number of virgins, just like the fewer belly dancers adorning their seats. There's also fewer jewels on the crowns. And finally, when my freckled-faced neighbor is called, he only walks away with a tiny island, twenty-five women, and his crown sports a sprig of small leaves and a single red ruby about the size of a dime.

I wait, a little excited despite the conflicting feelings zipping around in my head about Clay and the fact they're tossing people around like currency. I'll just add those to my list of things to unpack later. When I'm alone. And holy hell, I need some time alone to sort through this all soon or my head's going to explode like a lemon in a microwave. (Tried that once as a kid with my sisters. What. A. Mess.)

Zeus holds up his goblet of elixir once again.

It's my turn.

"Let us celebrate," he booms as the newly appointed kings of their territories raise their goblets high. "Drink, eat, and then the hunters amongst you may join me for the hunt. The horses and the hounds have been readied for our pleasure."

I blink.

The applause starts but dies quickly as Ladron steps past me to stand at the base of the pool. He raises his voice and points at me. "There is one kingdom more yet to be given this day."

Really, I'm fine. I don't want the scrutiny. After Professor Mandlin's class, I prefer less limelight. I grimace and wink at him in the effort to telegraph I can just find out later.

But he already has Zeus' attention. The god's head turns and his gaze sweeps my direction.

I hunch down in my couch, feeling just like I had in college.

"Timothy?" Zeus thunders.

The purple-robe wearing man we met before hurries to Zeus' side. There's a quick consultation, and then, the god is booming, "Come forward…Lily."

Lily. Just Lily. With all the -ethsus and -ethnes running around, the name sounds so out of place. I stand on wobbly legs, and right myself, sucking in a deep breath and crossing my fingers in hopes that this won't end as badly as my encounters with Professor Mandlin.

As I arrive, Zeus descends from his throne to meet me. "Let me see your palm," he says, his voice no less imposing this close up. If I didn't know better, I'd say Zeus has something of a god complex, with all his booming and bombasting.

I extend my hand, feeling even more like a shrimp than usual. I'm used to people towering over me, but these guys are bigger than most, and Zeus is the biggest so far. Up close, he is a pillar of muscle with a neck as thick as a tree trunk. His arms are beyond ridiculous, but I guess that's what you get from tossing lightning bolts around for fun. They're probably heavier than they look.

"There's a mystery here," his bass rumbles deep as he squints at my palm.

Mystery? He might as well have said mistake. I feel deflated. So, I'm not a goddess, after all?

Zeus frowns, and then he straightens and raises his goblet. "A divine being, but which one remains hidden," he announces to the crowd. "Doubtless, of borderline divinity."

There's scattered, polite applause.

Zeus turns his attention back to me. "Perhaps your past will become clearer, in time. Until we know your proper name, we'll call you by your earthly one. Lily."

That's fine by me. I like my name.

"Your kingdom, then," he continues, looking a bit bored. Timothy thrusts a scroll into his hands, and he runs his finger down the length, stopping at the bottom. "Upon you, Lily, I shall bestow the land south of the River Eurotas, the Land of the Dungeons."

"That's absurd," the words erupt from Ladron's mouth before anyone has a chance to clap.

I glance over my shoulder and see he's standing right behind me.

"Absurd?" Zeus' voice turns overly quiet. "Dare you question me?"

I hold my breath, and from the complete stillness in that great hall, it seems like everyone else does, too. Every eye is wide, every jaw dropped.

Ladron doesn't let that bother him, though. Apparently the only one who doesn't care about Zeus' displeasure, he forges ahead. "The dungeons are hardly a kingdom fit for a goddess."

Zeus snorts and folds his arms. "Perhaps she should have attended the ceremony at Hera's, then?"

There are a few laughs and I want to melt through the stone floor. It's Professor Mandlin 2.0, the Greek God version. I feel the heat on my cheeks.

But Ladron doesn't back down. "She deserves a fine queendom, fertile lands, servants—"

"She'll take what I bestow," Zeus roars. His voice echoes through the great room and ends in a crack of thunder. "The Dungeons. A servant. And two harem members. Torak, Son of Poseidon and Mirk, Son of Hades."

I blink. *Harem* members? So I hadn't misheard. This…is awkward. What the hell am I going to do with a harem?

I mean…besides the obvious.

Ladron is scowling. "This must be some kind of blunder," he objects, pointing to the scroll. "Bastard sons?" He nods over his shoulder at Mirk standing behind my couch. "And Torak's not even here. What kind—"

"You think to question me?" Zeus tosses his head, and I swear I see electricity snapping in his eyes. I step back, half expecting him to toss out a thunderbolt and roast me alive.

He leaves his dais to stalk directly over to Ladron. "Perhaps, then, you'd prefer to stand in Torak's place?"

A horrified murmur ripples through the crowd.

Zeus is angry. Really angry. And as new as I am, I know this can't be good. "Thanks," I say. Thanks? To a god? I clear my throat and try again. "I am grateful and honored—"

They don't even hear me. Ladron's staring Zeus straight in the eye. "I'd prefer you made things right."

That elicits a deep scowl from Zeus. He juts his

jaw, his beard protruding straight out of his chin. "You dare question me?"

"No, not really," I say, trying again to be heard. I fail. I might as well be a flea, and standing so close to these gigantic men, I actually feel like one.

"I simply seek justice," Ladron says. "A divine being has returned, one of enough stature that their name is written on *your* scroll."

Zeus' face darkens. He's obviously pissed, and it's not about me anymore but Ladron. "You risk your wealth, your position, to question *me?*" He's outraged. "So be it. You shall forsake your lands and join Lily in the Dungeons—as a member of her harem."

Mine is one of the collective gasps that circle the room.

Ladron draws himself to his full height, which is immense. I barely come up to his shoulders. He bellows to Zeus, "I would be honored."

Zeus takes that news as about as well as a cat tossed into a swimming pool. He throws the scroll at Ladron, who ducks. It rolls and lands in the center pool, floats a second, and then sinks with a soft plop.

Furious, Zeus grabs the silver circlet that Timothy's holding and reaches over to jam it unceremoniously on my head.

It's too big and slides down over my eyebrows, tipping a little to one side.

"Go," Zeus thunders. Then, he turns to Ladron again. "And you, you'll take only the clothes on your back."

Ladron nods stiffly.

But Zeus is already ignoring him and returns to his throne. He sits, raises his hand and the feast begins, with Clay by his side, laughing and drinking together like they've known each other forever.

The music blares as I scoot back to my couch as fast as I can with Ladron right behind me. As we arrive, Mirk claps his hands with an exaggerated slowness. "Welcome to the harem, Lord *Ladron*," he says, his every syllable a sexy rumble that drips in dark amusement.

There it is again. Harem. Surely, it doesn't mean what I think it does. Maybe it's a ceremonial position of some kind? I'll have to find out. Later. Right now, my elderly servant is offering me a platter of fruit, muttering to himself about something "unnatural." I take a handful of grapes, sit down, and motion for Ladron to join me.

"You shouldn't have given up everything," I say.

The couch dips under his weight, nearly sending me tumbling against his strong thigh. God, he's gorgeous. Why had Zeus said 'harem?' Now, my mind threatens to go places it shouldn't—like it needed the help between Ladron and Mirk oozing all the sexiness.

I clear my throat and jerk my gaze back to his, but I forget what I planned to say and just notice how unusual his eyes are. They're different, once you're this close. Blue, yes, but there's a ring of green in the center. And his lashes are very dark—pitch black, actually—for a blond. And long...

He's staring at me, and I realize with a start that we were chatting about something else. Right? Oh. "You can't give up everything. That nice house you have on the hill, and—"

"Luxuries mean nothing," he says, his lean jaw clenched.

I'm not sure I agree. I've had so few luxuries that I cherish each one—or at least I did before I died. But I'm not going to press the point. Especially not here.

Around us, the feast has started in earnest. Platter after heaping platter of artfully arranged delicacies are carried by, my servant snagging me servings from each as best he can. He's not very fast, so he misses every other one, but I don't mind. My stomach has soured to food after Zeus' treatment, though I do enjoy the pancakes soaked in honey and sprinkled with sesames seeds. And, of course, the lemon nut cake.

Ladron and Mirk don't eat. Mirk keeps to the back and lurks there, watching the scene before him like he's taking mental notes. For what? The more I watch, the more Hades' son intrigues me. Several times, he catches me staring at him—and his bulging biceps—and even though I try to withstand his gaze, I can't. About three seconds into our contest, something enters his eyes, something that just oozes raw sensuality, and I avert my gaze before I can stop myself. It's automatic.

Halfway through the feast, Hera and her new goddesses arrive, and the belly-baring virgins take their dancing and scarf-twirling next level. It's a madhouse after that, but an entertaining one. Some of the gods leave with Zeus for the hunt. Others remain, including myself, and when everyone that's left crowds around a stunning goddess with silver-blonde hair, I inch closer myself. Turns out she's Aphrodite, and I fangirl a bit when I realize she was a famous YouTube star. I was a follower of her channel and mourned with the rest of her fans when we recently found out she'd died in a car crash.

Ladron and Mirk tail me everywhere, and I can't decide if I feel like a celebrity with bodyguards or a prisoner escorted by police. I chat with the other newly crowned royalty, or I try. When I'm not ignored, I get a lot of sympathy over my kingdom and allotments. Not even one gift, they keep saying with a sad shake of their heads.

The fourth time I hear that, I decide I'm done for the night, but before I can escape, I see Clay coming toward me. I make a hard left and slip into a circle gathered around the newly returned Thanatos.

"Tomorrow," he's saying, "I've requested a quadriga with white horses for the journey."

"I've reserved the chestnuts, myself. For the ride to my fleet," my freckle-faced companion—Hymenaios, the God of Weddings—responds. He grins when he sees me and asks, "And you?"

"Me, what?" I ask, staring up at them all. They're all well over six feet, and I'm disappointed. I'd have thought I'd have come back at least a few inches taller, being a goddess and all.

"Your transportation to claim your kingdom," Thanatos supplies. "We leave here tomorrow."

"Didn't get the memo," I say.

"I'm sure your servants—er, servant—did," Hymenaios declares. "Just join the rest of us here at dawn."

"Thanks," I say, and deciding the coast is clear, I sneak off.

Only, I get no further than a few feet, when a figure steps out of a group of dancers and blocks my path.

"Lily," he says.

I scowl. "Clay."

7

"TRUE WISDOM COMES to each of us when we realize how little we understand about life, ourselves, and the world around us." ~Socrates

MY FORMER CRUSH-TURNED-TRAITOR IS ALL spiffy in his fancy Greek tunic with a golden crown of leaves on his head. Just why he deserved that—after shoving someone into the path of hellhounds—I'll never understand. I scowl, but I know I'll have to confront him eventually.

Still. I'm not going to ignore that particular elephant stampeding in the room. "You have a lot of nerve," I say.

"Turned out pretty well for you, didn't it?" he

asks, as if he's done me a favor. "The Greek Classic obsessed girl gets to live her dream. Oh, boohoo."

I ball my hands into fists to keep from slapping him. "You're an ass." Because of him, my family is crying their hearts out right now. I grit my teeth, fighting my own tears as I force emotions back into the box that I shoved them. I can't think of my family, not right now. They will undo me.

"Not sure how you wrangled your name onto the 'Gods Returned' list," Clay says with a superior smirk. "But you only got yourself shafted. You should've played by the rules. The goddesses are all pairing up with newly made kings, and even the worst of the lot's getting a far better deal than you did."

"Oh, I see. My dream is to be wife material?" Was he always this chauvinistic? Was I just too blind to see it? He couldn't have been that good of an actor. "No, thanks. I'm more than happy with being the Dungeon Queen." And suddenly tired of the whole thing—and above all, him—I turn around to Ladron and Mirk. "Let's go."

Ladron nods, and Mirk's shoulders relax in what looks like outright relief. I guess he's not a fan of feasts. Given how wildly successful my first one has been—pffft—I don't blame him.

We navigate through the celebrations and finally

make our way back to the main entrance where it all began. I stare up at the night sky, at the stars so different than any I've ever seen, and in the stillness of the night, with the strains of music fading in the distance, the magnitude of my loss loosens the last threads of resistance I can muster.

I died.

Which means I'm never going home.

Tears burn my eyes, but I blink them away. If I dive too deeply into thoughts of my family... well, I can't. Not yet. Not here. I choke back a sob and frantically search for a change of subject.

"We leave for the Dungeons in the morning, right?" I ask. "Are we supposed to meet up here?"

"Yes," Ladron replies a bit absently. He seems distracted. "I'll make the necessary arrangements."

"Sounds good," I say. "Then, it's off to bed."

They both give me a look I can't interpret, until I recall the word 'harem', and all the awkward confusion returns with a rush. My cheeks warm with embarrassment as I look away, only to find myself glancing down at their crotches. This is...not better.

Could it get anymore awkward?

Short answer: yes.

Because the next second, I blurt, "Where are we sleeping?" And then I feel compelled to clarify, "Me, I mean. Alone. I'm sleeping alone. Of course, you're sleeping, too. Somewhere… else…"

The dark fae just stands there, but I swear his eyes glint in amusement and with a smoky kind of sensuality I want to swim in.

Which does nothing to diffuse this increasingly uncomfortable conversation.

"There's a matter of unfinished business, first," Ladron says, kindly ignoring my flustered, one-sided exchange. "This way."

He stalks off, and I take a few steps, but Mirk doesn't follow, so I hesitate, waiting.

After a few paces, Ladron notices he's the only one headed off, and he turns back, arching an annoyed brow at Mirk.

"I follow only my lady's command," Mirk says, clearly using me as an excuse to toy with Ladron.

I swallow a sigh. I'll have to find out what's up with them, but later. Right now, I'm done with conflict and drama. I just want to crawl into bed and let my tears flow. So, I step between them before they can escalate any further and ask Ladron, "What unfinished business?"

His eyes shift from Mirk to me and his face softens. "It's Torak, Son of Poseidon. He's a member of your harem by Zeus' command, and that means he is bound to you. We should find him tonight since we're leaving at dawn."

Another one? "About this harem...explain please?"

Both men straighten a little, and though they don't answer in words, their mannerisms say it all. Mirk studies me with a half-hooded expression, his eyes full of dark promise, and Ladron's gaze is bold and warm, sweeping my imagination into a sun-drenched dance where clothing is optional.

Right. So it really is *that* kind of harem. I have no inbox for this, no life experience or script to fall back on, so I change the subject instead, mentally filing this into my 'think about later' box. "Do you guys know where this Torak even is?"

"One of three places," Mirk supplies dryly, his lip curling in one corner. "All involving wine."

"Is he even worth bothering about?" I ask, uneasy with the so-called-harem I already seem to have. "We've quite the journey ahead of us tomorrow, don't we?" It's going to be hard enough with the elderly, arthritic servant—tomorrow, I silently vowed to learn his name—and it didn't seem wise to throw in a rabble-rousing drunk, as well.

"He's a shifter," Ladron replied. "In the Dungeons he'll be quite useful."

"A shifter?" I repeat. There aren't too many shifters and fae in the Greek Mythological legends I've read, and certainly not any silver-eyed ones wearing tight leather leggings. Of course, at just the thought of his leggings I find myself ogling Mirk's muscled thighs again. It seems death has made me quite the horny lemon.

"Torak is the offspring of Poseidon's mating with the She-Wolf of Foloi Forest," Mirk says.

When I gain control of my eyes and meet his again, I see a glint of amusement there. Oh, he's noticed my obsession with his…assets. There's no doubt.

I clear my throat. "She-Wolf? The Greek gods sleep with anything, don't they?" I end with a nervous laugh and switch subjects. "Let's just go round him up real quick, shall we?"

"This way." Ladron waves us down the hill.

As I follow, Mirk falls into step beside me. My eyes sneak a peek at his sinewy thighs before I can stop them. "I haven't heard of the fae in Greek Legends before," I say, forcing my gaze straight ahead.

"We are new arrivals to this world," he says. "We've settled in the north and rarely leave."

"Oh?" I never gave my thought to an evolving Greek mythos. It was always something in the past. In myth and legend. Now, I'm part of it, and I realize with a start that like any civilization, it would of course change with time. "Why did you leave, then?"

He arches a brow. "It's not wise to ignore a Zeus summons."

Ah, the harem thing again. "Torak did," I mutter.

"Here," Ladron interrupts, pointing to a tavern a little ahead to the right.

We look inside, but the place is mostly empty, with no wolf shifter to be found. We continue down the road and head for the beach.

In the distance, the baying of the hounds and the sound of a horn announces the return of the hunt. I pause and glance back at the mountain looming high behind us, alive with twinkling lights and then gaze back at the blue water, now reflecting the night sky above, dotted with stars and the city lights. It's a strange world I'm in, but a beautiful one.

As we arrive at the second tavern, the door flies open, and a bearded man is ejected onto the street to sprawl at our feet. As he struggles to rise, I see he's sporting a paunch for a belly and he's missing two teeth. I wince, half convinced he's Torak, but when Ladron doesn't react to him, I release a silent breath of relief and watch him stagger off, belching.

"Now, *this* is Torak's sort of place," Mirk's sarcastic

voice quips as he steps up to the door. There, he pauses and glances back at me, "You might want to wait outside. It's rough here."

I toss my head. I'm a goddess. I can handle a few drunk men. I push past him and stride in confidently.

The center of the room is cleared with the patrons divided on either side of the house. All eyes are on two men who circle each other in the center.

One man is a red-haired, oversized mountain of muscle, but it's the other man that steals my breath away. He's dazzling. His brown hair is long, wavy, and braided at the temples, and he's dressed like a gladiator, wearing only double-shouldered pauldrons with a harness and a leather-paneled war skirt. Bands of muscle ripple over his chest and arms, and even at this distance, the green of his eyes stand out in sharp contrast to his dark hair, practically glowing like emeralds.

As people shout their bets, Mirk chuckles behind me, "As expected. Torak, himself."

I turn to see him pointing straight at the stunning gladiator, and my heart does another flop. Obviously, in the afterlife, gorgeous men are as common as chickweed.

Someone whistles, signaling the fight to begin, but Torak holds up a hand and with a cheeky grin, detours to the bar to down a pot of wine. The house erupts in cheers, egging him on as he chugs it down, and after wiping his mouth with the back of his hand, he's back in the ring.

"It's a fool who fights drunk," his opponent booms with a wicked laugh.

Torak wiggles his brows.

I join Mirk who slouches against the wall to watch the fight while Ladron stays by the door. He folds his arms, looking slightly put out, but then, he's a musician, so I can see how physical fighting isn't really his thing.

Turns out, he doesn't have to suffer long.

The whistle no sooner shrills before Torak's fist moves quicker than sight. There's a sickening sound of bone on bone.

The next instant, his mountain-of-muscle opponent is flat on the floor, out cold.

The left side of the room erupts into cheers.

Torak straightens, and when his gaze lands on me, he stills and just stares. I can't help but stare back. His magnetism pulls me in. Unlike Mirk, whose smoldering sensuality is so intense that I'm the first to look away, with Torak, I just fall into those green eyes as if into a refreshing pond on a hot day. They bore into my soul, as if he's reading my every thought. Everything else in the room fades away, and I only see him as he slowly stalks toward me, like a predator hunting its prey. His leather war skirt slides over his thighs, and his chest ripples beneath the harness.

He stops a few inches from me, our bodies so close I can feel the heat emanating from his skin. He bows over my hand, his breath warm on my skin as his lips nearly graze my flesh. My stomach drops in anticipation.

"You were missed at the feast," Ladron says, ruining the moment.

"And?" Torak prompts. He straightens, but his gaze never leaves my face.

Mirk's lip curls with a dark amusement I don't understand. "This is your mistress."

Torak lifts a brow and this time, he does kiss my hand, his full, sensuous lips practically branding my skin, which prickles at the contact. My pulse quickens with my breath, and his brow lifts, just enough to let me know he's quite aware of his effect on me.

"You know I don't take orders from Zeus," Torak says. Then his gaze bores into mine. "It's nothing personal."

It feels personal, and I'm not sure what to do. I'm certainly not going to order him to join me…harem. Gods, I can't even think the word without cringing.

I straighten my back and nod. "Very well. Let's not waste more time here, then," I say, turning away.

But Ladron steps forward and pulls Torak to the side. He leans in and whispers something in the warrior's ear, and Torak scowls.

When Ladron is done speaking, Torak sighs. "Fine."

He stalks over to me. "I am at your service, m'lady." He bows formally with more grace than I would have expected, then winks at me.

Surrounded by three veritable gods in a rowdy tavern that smells—let's just say questionable—it's getting hard to breathe.

I shift uncomfortably. "Let's get some rest," I glance at the three sexy men, hoping gods need sleep too. "We've an early day tomorrow, don't we?"

"I'll make arrangements," Ladron offers. "There's a suitable inn up the street."

I follow him out of the tavern with Mirk and Torak trailing behind. I'm keenly aware of Torak's almost possessive gaze drinking me in, and I'm unsettled by my own reaction as heat pools in my belly and a new kind of need builds up in me.

For anyone who's keeping score, I'm now officially attracted to three of the three men I've met since arriving here, which further supports my hypothesis that becoming a goddess has made me horny as hell.

Looking for a distraction from Torak, my gaze lands on Ladron, who's striding a few paces ahead of me, and it's super hard to ignore the way the moonlight paints his blond hair a blue-tinted silver. But while he might be a distraction from Torak, he's definitely not helping put out the fire that's growing inside. The two men are very different. Torak is raw, brute strength, and Ladron is so classy, the personification of elegance and polish, with the soul of a poet and the hands of a musician. Just looking at him sends the butterflies swarming in my stomach.

Expelling a breath, I glance sideways at Mirk, Hades' bastard son, the ultimate bad boy, but a mystery in his own right. He's a scorching kind of hot. And, as usual, he senses my eyes on him and turns his head to look at me, full on. I can't take the intensity I see burning there—even from the side—and drop my gaze to the play of his muscled thighs under that laced leather.

I expel a breath and force my eyes ahead. So much for distractions. I'm flooded with a sizzling inner heat and my cheeks burn as I focus my gaze on Zeus' great palace high above us. It stands out like a blazing torch in the night, every one of its magnificent windows alight.

The sight dampens my excitement, reminding me again that I've died...and what my family is going through.

And suddenly, I'm cold inside.

Melanie. Sarah. Mom. Dad.

I'm swept into memories. Of all the laughter. The forts in the summer. Dad's constant snoring. Mom's recipes. The past rises up to consume the present. I scarcely notice Ladron leading me into an inn a few cuts above where we just were, with stone rather than dirt floors, and not a single brawling patron.

Mirk and Torak secure our rooms as I walk in a daze, the weariness of the day arriving all at once to bury me in layers of pain that feel heavier with each step.

I bite my lip, accepting Ladron's arm when I nearly trip walking up a wide staircase that leads to an open, airy room.

The moment I look at the bed, I burst into tears, the finality of it all hitting me too hard to ignore this time.

I can't Skype my sisters and tell them about the craziness of this world. They would melt hearing about my new harem of breathtaking gods.

And my dad. I'll never get one of his bear hugs again.

Or spend Sunday morning doing crosswords with my mom.

The sobs wrack my body, and I can't stop. Can't breathe. Can't suppress the pain any longer.

"This, too, shall pass," Ladron murmurs as he folds me into his arms and guides us to the bed, where I cling to him like he's all I've got.

Another wave of grief washes over me as I realize that's not entirely untrue. I don't know anything about this new life I'm heading into. All I have are him, Mirk and Torak. Three men who yesterday were strangers. Hell, yesterday they were less than strangers. They were myths.

It takes me some time before I can breathe normally again, and by then Ladron and I are stretched out on the bed, my head resting against his warm, broad chest.

Gradually, I become aware of him stroking my hair, and I close my swollen eyes. My eyelids feel like sandpaper. And I'm so tired.

"Rest, *Lilyitsa*," Ladron whispers into my hair. "Tomorrow is a new day."

Lilyitsa… His Greek endearment of 'itsa' comforts me but at the same time, it only drives the point home. I really am in a foreign place and I'm never going back to the Lemon family cottage. The thought summons a fresh bout of tears and I hiccup against Ladron's reassuring warmth until finally, truly exhausted, I close my eyes and let sleep take me.

[8]

"APPLY yourself both now and in the next life. Without effort, you cannot be prosperous. Though the land be good, You cannot have an abundant crop without cultivation." ~ Plato

"IT'S TIME TO AWAKEN, *LILYITSA*," A SOOTHING baritone slips through my dreams.

I lift my lashes, confused for a moment. I'm lying on a bed facing a window with gauzy curtains and a dazzling view of the Mediterranean. The sheets are soft and… I'm not alone.

I turn into the embrace of a beautiful man with golden curls and kind eyes, and all the memories—and heartache—flood back into me.

There's a sympathetic smile on Ladron's lips as he strokes my head. "Good morning. I wanted to let you sleep as long as possible."

I shift in bed, peeling my body away from his, and I instantly miss the warmth and comfort his presence brought me. Rubbing my eyes, I yawn and look around. "This is all real. I wasn't dreaming." It's not a question, and I'm not entirely surprised, but it's still a shock to be dead and in a Greek afterlife as a god—er, goddess rather. If I were a god I'd be treated with a lot more respect it seems. I'm thinking that'll take a few days to really settle.

"It wasn't a dream. And unfortunately, we haven't much time to dally now," Ladron says, standing and stretching his long, lean muscles. "My father suffers from a distinct lack of patience."

I look up at him and feel my cheeks flush at how close we've been all night—physically and emotionally. "Thank you," I say. "I…I didn't want to be alone last night, and somehow you knew that."

He reaches out and traces my cheekbone with his thumb. "No one should have to process that kind of grief alone. If I could carry your pain for you, know that I would."

I close my eyes and savor the feel of his touch for just a moment longer before forcing myself to think ahead to the day. "You mentioned your father. Which one was he?"

Ladron tenses, his gaze pulling away from mine. "Zeus."

"Zeus. As in *the* Zeus?" I gasp as my knowledge of Greek mythology clicks together with the reality I'm living. "Your father is *Zeus?*"

The corner of his lip curls into a bitter smile. "The one and only."

Of course, it's been over a thousand years. Zeus would have sons I haven't heard of, but I'm still shocked. As Zeus' son—bastard or not—he is royalty and held in high esteem. I stare at him in wonder. "That means...you gave up a lot to come with me. Your palace, your wealth, your standing. Why? If the condolences I got last night are any indication, it doesn't sound like my new queendom has much to offer."

He shrugs. "I've been quite bored of late. It's high time for adventure." He takes my hand to help me off the bed.

"Yeah, but Zeus is your *father*," I repeat. I'm going to have a hard time getting over that.

He hesitates, and part of me instantly regrets pushing back so much. I mean, of course I want him tagging along. He's gorgeous, kind, and sexy. And even though I've only known him for a short period of time, he just *feels* right.

"I have a confession," he says, his voice rumbles low and his eyes begin to dance with amusement.

His reaction is puzzling. "What's so funny?"

"Strictly speaking, my name isn't Ladron. It's rather a nickname." The laughter in his eyes deepens. "As for my given name, you might be familiar with it: Hermes."

He drops that bomb so casually, that it takes a few seconds to make the connection. Hermes. Oh. My. God. *Hermes.* Of all the Greek gods, I crushed on Hermes the most. I've spent more time than I'll ever admit secretly daydreaming your standard sexy god scenarios like him swooping down from the sky wearing his winged helmet, whispering pickup lines as he whisks me away. Fun, corny ones like "The only seat above first class is my lap," and the more romantic "Hello, I'm a thief and I'm here to steal your heart." He was a master thief, after all.

"Ladron," I blurt, full realization dawning. Ladron. Master thief. "Clever."

He shrugs.

I stare, still stuck on the fact he's…*Hermes.* Then, I feel my cheeks flush hot, like somehow, he already knows about all those silly pickup lines. "Why didn't you tell me from the beginning?" I ask, mostly to distract myself from just what those daydreams had been about...

"At the time, you were still struggling with where you were. Who you were," he answers as sympathy replaces the amusement on his face. "I didn't want to make that journey even more complicated for you."

God, who knew Hermes would be so empathetic. Sexy *and* sensitive? What a devastating combo. I bite my lip and force my thoughts back to business. "So, should I start calling you Hermes now?"

As his name rolls off my lips I realize... *Hermes is in my harem?* This is so wrong. Wow, Zeus must really be pissed. And harem... Well, setting *that* aside for a second, Hermes in my queendom? The land of the Dungeons? He doesn't belong in such a—

His laugh breaks into my thoughts.

"You're not listening," he says when I glance up at him.

I wince apologetically. "Sorry. It's just..." I wave my hands at him. "Hermes, you know. He was always my favorite." The words just leave my mouth on their own. And when I realize what I've said I want to cringe.

"Favorite?" A gleam returns in those blue eyes.

I clear my throat. "Hermes, I—"

"No, please." He cuts me short by stepping closer. "I've grown fond of Ladron. If you want the truth, I'm weary of being trapped in my gilded cage. I'm ready to escape. Ready to seek new adventure. Ready to stretch my wings, as it were." He drops his voice into a near whisper and I'm so close, I swear I can feel his chest vibrate as he adds, "People change. Even Greek gods."

I stare up at him, still stunned by his confession as my brain struggles to reconcile the Greek myth with the very real flesh and blood man standing before me.

His gaze softens.

"And though we've only just met, I felt a connection to you the moment you appeared in my life. I couldn't let him banish you to the Dungeon lands alone."

"I have Mirk and Torak," I whisper, our lips so close now it's hard to think of anything but how his might feel pressed against my own.

His gaze drops to my mouth and his cheeks crease with a smile. "Like I said, I couldn't let you go alone."

Time stretches before us and I can feel the tension deepen as he slowly dips his head to bring his lips to mine, but just before the connection is made, there's a knock at the door. A serving maid barges into my room with two men carrying a tub, followed by a parade of young boys lugging buckets full of steaming water.

She pauses when she realizes she's interrupted us, but she doesn't leave. She just bows. "Your bath, m'lady."

"Uh, thanks." I take a step back from Ladron, the moment broken, and he grins. "I'll leave you to it then, my Queen. We will await your presence downstairs."

He takes my hand and brushes a kiss against it before disappearing out the door.

I'VE BEEN SOAKING IN THE HEAVEN OF A ROSE-petal milk bath so long the water has turned cold, my mind spinning with how close Ladron—Hermes!—and I came to kissing. I can still feel the warmth of his lips grazing mine, and the heat pooling in me stirs up a yearning that's only been growing since I woke up in his palace.

But I know I cannot continue to linger, so I reluctantly crawl out of the bath and dress myself in the decidedly non-Greek outfit that was left for me—one that I never knew I needed until now. The deep gray silk shirt feels so soft against my skin, and the black leather leggings with the knee-high boots give me a sense of command—and a few extra inches that I appreciate. The laces up the sides of the leggings make me wonder if Mirk had a hand in this—it seems his style. Maybe it's fae inspired? As I shrug into the high-low cut coat, I grin. This ensemble makes me feel powerful and strong as befits a Queen of the Dungeon, plus it's perfect for traveling. Win-win.

When I arrive downstairs, Ladron is staring out a window, lost in thought as Mirk balances a chair back on its two legs at the table. Torak is leaning against a counter, guzzling a pint of ale—figures. He seems to metabolize alcohol at an alarming rate.

When I enter, three heads turn in my direction, and I can't deny the pleasure I feel at the way they look at me. Ladron smiles, his face full of admiration. Torak looks ready to eat me, and I flush hot at *that* mental image. And Mirk's gaze nearly melts my leggings off.

I clear my throat to diffuse some sexual tension, then grab an apple off the tray in the center of the table. I pause, looking at the fruit with curiosity. "Do we need to eat?" I ask. "I'm habituated to it, but I just realized I'm not hungry in the way I used to be."

Ladron raises an eyebrow. "You and I have no need for food," he says. "We can survive without any, though we eventually will feel—off—if we go too long. You will discover the longer you are here, the more your body adapts to your goddesshood." He glances at Mirk and Torak. "They are not full gods, so have some consistent need of sustenance, but much less than a human."

"I'm going to have a lot of questions," I say, then bite into my apple.

Ladron smiles. "I am available for any and all of your needs," he says, his voice laden with layers of promise. "There are many perks to godhood that I would be happy to show you."

Flames rise in my cheeks and I clutch my apple as I straighten my spine. "That's good to know. We should get going now. As I understand it, Zeus doesn't like to be kept waiting." I head to the door, but I've taken no more than a step before another question pops in my mind. "You know, I'm curious about something."

Ladron tilts his head slightly to the side and the silent lift of his brows invites me to continue.

"Just why am I dealing with Zeus instead of Hera?" I mean, Aphrodite the YouTuber and the other goddesses had gone to Hera's feast. "Why was I singled out for all the Zeus fun? The only female there?"

"Your name appeared on his scroll." He says with a shrug, as if that explains everything.

"Got it."

But of course I don't 'got it.' For every question I ask, three more pop into my head. But, I know those will have to wait their turn if we have any hope of getting on the road in a timely fashion.

Taking another bite from my apple, I head for the door.

The guys rise to follow, and as I pass Mirk, he murmurs, "The outfit suits you well, my lady."

My lady? I pause and look at him. His shirt is open at the collar and the glimpse of the snake tattoo I'd seen before is gone. In its place is a complicated Celtic pattern, one with swirls running tantalizingly under his jaw. I draw a breath and force my eyes to meet his. Today's a new day, isn't it? Today, I'll look him in the eye and win. "The clothes are lovely," I say. "Fae? I was wondering if you had something to do with the selection."

"They are, indeed, fae," he says, and then leans closer. "You seemed to like the leggings. I've noticed you staring at mine."

The provocative glint dancing in those silver eyes of his makes me flush, and I look away...at his muscular thighs, again.

I spin on my heel and stride out the door to break the lure the delicious fae seems to have over me.

Outside, I pause and soak in the sunshine, again admiring the view of the blue-tiled roofs plunging to the Cerulean blue sea. Two fleets of ships anchored during the night. One a mighty black-sailed war fleet, spreading out over the eastern horizon. The other much smaller, about one-fourth the size of the war fleet, with ships of the merchant class variety, single-decked with blue-and-white striped sails.

"Epimetheus' ships," Ladron says, joining me to nod at the black warships.

I roll my eyes. Of course. Clay, again. What a way to ruin the morning. "I hadn't realized he needed ships with a land-locked kingdom," I say under my breath.

Ladron smirks at my salty attitude. "Epimetheus left his war fleet in the care of Alpheus," he says. "To be reinstated upon his return."

The word 'reinstated' arrests my attention. "You mean he left his ships like in storage? He knew he was coming back? Like some kind of insurance policy?"

Ladron smiles. "All of the gods come back, sooner or later."

This news piques my interest. What do I have out there? An island with white sand beaches? A city on the edge of the sea surrounded by orange and lemon groves? And what about artifacts? What had I collected during my many years as a goddess?

For the first time, I feel a genuine excitement over what could be my real history. "So, I would have left my own legacy behind, somewhere," I say. Something that is mine, that identifies me and unlocks the past. A rich past, straight out of a Greek legend. I shiver as goosebumps pebble my flesh.

"Yes." Ladron chuckles. "And once we know for sure which goddess you are, your previous possessions will be returned."

He smiles, and I'm not thinking of possessions anymore, but the crinkle of his blue eyes and the fall of his tunic clinging to his chest. He was in my bed. I snuggled in his arms through the night...

But the thought of just why he was there, comforting me through my tears, dampens the rising heat. Which is fine. If I'm going to be traveling with these three gorgeous guys, muscles and beds are the last things I should focus on if we actually want to get anywhere.

It only takes a few minutes to make our way through the massive gates of Zeus' palace, which is abuzz with even more activity than the day before. Legions of servants are bustling around, readying an army of entourages destined for the newly crowned kings—and queen, of course.

But the talk around us seems more agitated than excited, and I strain to catch bits of the conversations circling.

"…glowing red eyes with teeth so sharp they can cut through gods."

"…heard they ripped apart a child in a nearby town."

"I heard one of the gods came back after being killed on Earth. I heard it was hellhounds that did it," says another, and I wonder if they're talking about me or Clay. Probably Clay.

I gasp and clutch Ladron's hand. "Hellhounds are on the loose here as well?" I ask. "Why? What happened?"

Ladron frowns. "I've only heard rumors," he says. "But it seems another trio of beasts escaped and are causing some problems in local villages."

"As well as other things," Mirk mutters so softly I can hardly hear him.

My throat goes dry as I imagine innocent people dying such a grisly death, but then, Mirk's words register. "Other things?" The men exchange looks, concerned ones, so I prod, "What aren't you telling me?"

Ladron answers first, "Monsters are escaping from your Dungeons. Beasts I haven't seen in centuries. Not since Prometheus sealed them deep inside. There's no other explanation other than the Dungeons have been breached."

My steps falter. Wow. My queendom is a real fixer-upper. I mean, I'm not the picky type at all. I've spent my life shopping at garage sales and searching for treasures at thrift stores. But subterranean dungeons leaking monsters is a whole new level on the upscale front. Before I can ask anything else, Ladron tugs me forward, Mirk and Torak keeping pace with us.

Chariots line the palace walls, grouped by color and design, some with lion's heads engraved in the wheel hubs, and others painted with naked warriors wearing plumed helmets. The horse of choice seems to be Arabian, primarily black and white ones. They prance, tossing their heads proudly as they're led to the chariots and harnessed while packs of golden-collared Cretan hounds bark at their feet.

"Hermes," a voice calls above the din.

That name still sends a shiver down my spine, and I cast an admiring glance at Ladron as he turns to address the still purple-robed Timothy holding a scroll in his hand, waving for us to join him.

"Your arrangements have been made," he says when we meet. "This way."

He sets off with a hurried step toward the west end of the palace, and we follow.

As Ladron and Timothy walk ahead, I turn to Mirk striding silently by my side. "How far away are these Dungeons, anyway?" I ask, looking straight into his eyes, determined this time not to turn red or glance away. I have more important things to focus on than the devilish fae's silver eyes. Like how monsters are escaping my Dungeons.

"At most, a day by chariot," he answers with an easy shrug.

"I hate to even waste that much time, but I suppose there's no getting around it." My palms are itching for the chance to settle into my new life, and figure out a way to seal those Dungeons up again.

After some time, Timothy stops, halting all of us in the process as he faces the fig trees and the garden beyond. "There," he says, his voice hoarse and his shoulders hunched as if he's trying to make himself small.

I look around, puzzled, and notice the similar look of confusion on the faces of my men.

Ladron goes still, and I see the muscle on his jaw twitch.

As I follow his line of sight, I hear Mirk's sharp intake of breath, and I understand.

Under a fig tree, about three yards from the palace wall, stands my gray-haired, grizzled servant. He's not surrounded by chariots. Oh no. Not even a single serviceable wagon. Hell, not even a wheelbarrow. He's alone, holding the reins of a donkey with a burlap sack tossed over its back.

Ladron looks ready to murder someone, and I can feel the wounded egos suffering around me, but I don't care about status or silly slights.

I care about the people dying to monsters.

I care about getting to my queendom as quickly as possible to stop said monsters.

And by the looks of that donkey and my trembling servant by his side, it's going to take a hell of a lot longer than a day's journey—which means a higher death toll while I'm making camp in the woods.

I'm starting my life as Queen out with quite the bang.

[9]

"He is a wise man who does not grieve for the things which he has not, but rejoices for those which he has."
~ *Epictetus*

No one moves... well, except the donkey. The small creature stands in the sun, flicking his ears and swishing his tail to scare away the flies, oblivious to the fact he's the center of attention.

Ladron remains perfectly still, his face composed, but I can see he's furious. So is Mirk. There's a dangerous glint in his silver eyes that makes me think he's already calculating revenge. As for Torak, he just stalks to the donkey, removes the sack and tosses it over one broad shoulder. Then, he nods for Alfio to hop on. He's practical.

Timothy clears his throat three times before he manages to croak, "You'll have to leave soon. The, um, the schedule." He jabs weakly at the scroll again. "We're running late. The others...the others..."

Ignoring him, Ladron turns to me and says in a deadly soft voice, "Wait here."

I open my mouth to ask him what he plans, but he's gone before I can get the first word out. Timothy bumbles after him, calling for him to slow down.

I heave a sigh and go to greet my servant and check out my donkey.

"Good morning, m'lady," Alfio says from his perch on the animal's back.

He moves as if to jump down, but I shake my head. "Just stay there." I smile. He obviously needs the ride more than I do.

I reach over to tickle the donkey under the chin. "You're kind of cute," I say, looking into his big, brown eyes, ringed with lashes at least an inch long. "I know a lot of girls who'd kill for those." Well, I used to, anyway.

"At least he's young and strong," Mirk mutters, joining me.

I'm still hoping we can find a faster route to my

new kingdom. Time is of the essence. "Can we rent a chariot?" I ask. With what, I don't know. Maybe they have some kind of a goddess-credit-card plan here? "It's just for a day. Can't be that expensive, can it?"

"There won't be a stable who will go against Zeus," Torak says, slouching against the palace wall watching us. For a moment, I'm distracted at the picture he makes. In his war-skirt outfit sans shirt, he's the perfect Abercrombie & Fitch model. He looks at me through his lashes that sultry, sexy way, like he's imagining all the things he's going to do once we're alone. His lips curl into a sensuous smile, and I can't help but grin like a fool at him.

Mirk casually strolls between us and blocks my view, replacing it with one equally as attractive. I shake my head to clear it, and focus on what matters. Having run out of ideas for getting to my land outside the obvious, I sigh. "Looks like we're walking. How long will that take us?"

Mirk shrugs. "About three days."

Of course it's three days. Would it even be my life if it didn't come in threes?

As much as I hate to delay our arrival so long just so Zeus can flex his muscles, there's a part of me that's excited to explore on foot this realm I grew up reading about. And the prospect of a three-day hike would have daunted the old Lily Lemon, but not the new me. Like Ladron promised, I feel even stronger today than yesterday. I smooth my leggings and flex my feet. My boots fit me like a second skin, and I'm sure I can walk for miles in them, even brand new. Trekking across the countryside will be an awesome way to acquaint myself with my new homeland.

"Which way are we heading?" I ask, and as he points to the southwest, I look out over rolling hills and mountains rising in the distance. The sea glistening so brilliantly blue below me gives me a new idea. "What about ships? Can we sail to the Dungeons instead?"

Mirk dashes that dream with an immediate, "No." He reads my scowl and adds, "There's not a ship that would sail within ten leagues of those lands, even if the mighty Zeus himself commanded it."

"The water is cursed," Torak says, shoving himself off the wall to join us near the donkey. The way his insanely huge muscles ripple as he walks wakes the primal, primitive part of me that wants to growl, grab him by his hair, and drag him to bed. But he shatters the mental image I'm beginning to paint with, "They say the sea is as black as pitch there, as foul as the land itself."

I twist my lips at the bitter taste filling my mouth. Just exactly what kind of land has Zeus given me?

Before I can fish for more information, Ladron returns. He's changed into a leather half cuirass, and he's strapped a shield onto his back and belted a sword around his waist. In his hands, he carries a spear, a sheathed sword attached to a belt, and a black bullwhip.

"Your weapons, *Lilyitsa*," he announces as he arrives.

"Weapons?" I'm startled. Butter knives are more my style, but as I look at them, they seem inexplicably familiar, like the fading memories of an old dream returning.

"Allow me." Ladron hands the spear to Mirk and gives the whip to Torak before stepping up to me. He's so close we're almost touching, and as the sweet, hot rush of longing shoots through me, he slides the belted sword around my waist. I'm extra aware of the way he splays his fingers over the base of my spine, and when I glance sharply up at him, he's studying my face, a sexy smirk curving his lips. My stomach tightens as the butterflies return. With Ladron, it's always butterflies.

But it's more than physical attraction. I feel bad. He's given up so much for me already. I can't bear him suffering humiliation, too, forced to leave his father's palace with only a donkey. "Can't we just sneak out the back way?" I ask.

Ladron shrugs with a wry smile. "Let Zeus play his games. They don't matter. And as for routes off this mountain, let's take the quickest. The main road." He pauses as amusement—and something I can't quite define—sparks in his eyes. "Let's be gone before he notices what he's missing, shall we?"

Defiance. That's what I see. Understanding dawns. "What have you done?" Maybe the golden-haired Ladron is more of a bad boy than he looks beneath all the suave elegance. I grin.

With a smirk he nods at each weapon in turn. "The Spear of Truth. The Blade of Destiny. The Mortal Coil."

I eye each weapon with wonder. I don't recall reading about any of them on the Wikipedia list of Greek Artifacts or any of my books. Just how much has this world evolved? So many discoveries lay ahead. So many things to experience, to learn. A thrill of excitement pulses through me.

"Where do they come from?" I ask eagerly. "What do they do?"

Ladron chuckles at my delight. "You're like a child attending her first Panathenaea," he teases and then turns serious. "These weapons will serve you well just as they are, a whip, a sword, and a spear."

I respond with a pointed look. "They're more than that," I insist. I can feel their power, like an electric charge that buzzes against my skin when I get near them.

Ladron shrugs. "If they are, then only Prometheus knows what their secrets might be. He gave them as gifts to my father, long ago, and they've been locked in a vault ever since." He takes the whip from Torak and places it in my hands.

The whip's energy races through me, a physical thing, like it's opening doors I know lead to a secret buried deep inside. Then, his words register. "A locked vault? You mean you *stole* these from Zeus?"

Ladron lifts a devilishly playful brow. "Stole? That's rather a strong word."

I shake my head at his boldness. "You certainly live up to your name of thief, ripping off the god of gods like that," I tease in turn.

Then, the weaponry consumes my attention. I hold the whip in one hand, and run the other over the sword's hilt, marveling at how my fingers mold around it so naturally. It's big, made for a much larger hand, yet I'm positive I can wield it with skill. I unsheathe the blade, the metal hissing as it leaves the scabbard. And as I expect, the sword is so balanced I can scarcely tell where I end and it begins. It's a thing of beauty, exquisitely crafted and inlaid with golden flames that fan up the blade, twisting into a pattern near the hilt that I swear looks like a lemon.

I sheathe the sword and move on to inspect the whip. It's a bullwhip and a heavy duty one, all black, braided leather. And like the sword, it feels so natural, even more familiar. Giving into the sensation, I step sideways, away from the men, and flick my wrist, aiming for a plump fig hanging down from the nearby tree.

Somehow, the aim is perfect, and the whip's crack echoes like a gunshot.

The donkey brays and bucks, and my servant yelps, scrambling to hold on. As Torak reaches to steady the beast, Mirk holds out his hand, catching the fig neatly in his palm.

"Sorry," I'm quick to apologize to my grizzled servant.

He grumbles something under his breath, something that sounds like "unnatural," but I'm too distracted by the spear that Mirk is offering me to really take notice.

The spear is stunning. Two golden dragons with rubies for eyes curl around the hilt to entwine partway down the shaft. I heft the weapon, tossing it in the air with a spin before catching it again, feeling as if I've done this thousands of times.

Through the trees and in the garden beyond, I see a statue of Epimetheus about fifty feet away. Someone's placed a woven crown of olive branches on his head. I grin. The angle is perfect. Letting instinct take over, I launch the spear, quicker than sight.

The spear sails through the air and shoots straight through the top of the crown, lifting the woven leaves off the statue's head before skimming to a stop on the wide expanse of grass stretching behind.

There. Take that, Clay.

I turn back to the men. And I like what I see.

Ladron watches me in open admiration. Mirk observes me from under hooded, sensual eyes. Torak grins.

As our eyes meet, he says, "I'll fetch it," before sprinting off.

"Shall we?" Ladron suggests, waving his hand at the gates. "Before the alarm sounds?"

"Yes, let's go," I say, eager to be off before someone discovers my new toys are missing.

After fetching the spear and strapping it to my back so that I feel like a total badass, we head for the gates. I honestly imagine this is how Xena: Warrior

Princess felt, and I'm here for it. I walk up front with Ladron, Mirk in the middle, and Torak bringing up the rear, leading the donkey and Alfio.

We push our way through the hordes of servants scrambling to ready their master's affairs. Everyone is so busy, they don't even look our way, and with each step, I'm beginning to think this won't end up so bad for Ladron, after all.

An impressive regiment of Greek warriors line the road ahead. The men gleam in chest plates adorned with dazzling six-pack abs, as red-plumed Corinthian helmets top their heads. Each man clutches a gold spear in the left, and in the right, a ram's horn, banded in gold and silver.

Several processions compete for space on the road, crowding each other as if they're planning to race out of the mighty gates. It's an utter madhouse, reminding me of freeway rush-hour traffic—only with chariots, donkeys, and belly dancers instead of pissed off people in cars. And then I hear it.

The roar.

A sound both man and beast. A sound that makes me think of cigarettes and exhaust-fumes. A sound that makes me feel dread.

I look over the crowds.

To an enormous metal cage at the edge of the

gates. Locked inside sits a giant creature, its upper body covered in skin, muscles bulging at unnatural angles, its lower body hidden in fur, hooves where feet should be. And when it turns to me, it meets my gaze with one single eye.

My frazzled mind can only muster one thought.

Cyclops.

"FOR A MAN TO conquer himself is the first and noblest of all victories." ~ Plato

"HOLY LEMONS, THAT'S A REAL CYCLOPS." I GASP. It's one thing to know the theory that all the myths and legends are real, it's quite another to actually see a real monster in the flesh. I mean, Hermes, Zeus and the others are still basically human. This thing isn't. "A *real* cyclops."

"They say Artemis' hunters captured it just outside the walls this morning," Mirk supplies in a low voice.

The men exchange guarded looks that pique my

curiosity, but before I can ask, the cyclops roars again and begins to bash itself against the cage.

I tense. "Is that thing going to hold?"

Ladron subjects the cage to a swift, calculating gaze before nodding. "There's nothing to fret over. It was made by Hephaestus himself. We used many such as these to trap the beasts in the Dungeons, securing the safety of the kingdoms."

I turn to him in surprise. "We? You worked on the Dungeons, too?" I mean, it makes sense. He's Hermes. He's been around for like, forever. A headache forms behind my eyes and I pinch the bridge of my nose and squint, trying to think. "You mentioned before monsters were escaping the Dungeons, but you didn't say how?"

"No one knows," Mirk cuts in. "They were supposed to be unbreakable."

"And Prometheus helped build them?"

"The Dungeons are his creation," Ladron said. "Some of us merely helped wrangle the monsters."

Merely. Right. That sounds like quite the task. "So what does the Dungeon Master himself say about all this? Does he have any idea why monsters are now escaping and terrorizing people on multiple worlds?"

The men exchange another look as Ladron replies, "Well, that's part of the problem."

"And?" I push. Something's obviously going on here between them.

"After Prometheus built the Dungeons and we cleaned up the countryside, Zeus betrayed him by locking him inside, at the very center," Ladron replies, the muscle clenching on his jaw announcing just what he thinks about that.

"Wow." I blink in surprise. Of all the Greek gods, Zeus has always been near the bottom of my *Likability List*. Now, he's falling off entirely. "Poor Prometheus." And poor us. "The one person who could help us fix this mess is trapped in the most dangerous place there is."

"Exactly," says Ladron. "Something needs to be done. Prometheus needs to be found. Zeus, Poseidon, and Hades avoid the issue at every turn. But now with the monsters stalking outside the walls, and some even finding their way to Earth, this is a matter they can no longer ignore."

I think of the hellhounds. "How do I get there?" At his puzzled look, I add, "Earth, I mean."

"You cannot."

I don't like his tone of finality. "The hellhounds clearly have, and there are plenty of stories about the Greek gods interacting with mortals and—"

"You cannot," Ladron repeats firmly. "Zeus forbade it, long ago."

Yeah, like who wants to listen to him right now? "So, there is a way. Technically."

"Technically, yes, but I will not help you," he says, his face hard, guarded. "Gods have caused mortals enough strife."

I think back to all the stories. The Trojan War. Athena transforming Medusa into a monster. Zeus creating Pandora and then tempting her to release evil into the human world. He might have a point, there. But, still. "If it's forbidden, how are monsters finding their way to Earth now then?"

This time, it's Torak who cuts a side-look at Ladron. So, all three of them know something, do they?"

"There's only one explanation," Mirk says, crossing his arms. "A god is behind this. Only their kind can open the paths between worlds."

"Their kind? Not yours?"

"Demigods don't have that power," he says. "Only a full god can do such a thing."

"Someone like Zeus. Poseidon. Hades," says Torak.

"Ladron…" I add, casting a glance at the god by

my side. "And me," I realize. My heart gives a little leap of joy. Maybe there's a way I can see my family again, after all.

"Don't try it," Ladron says quietly. "Believe me, nothing good will come if you do." There's something personal there. A long-buried pain in his eyes, his voice.

Mirk drops a hand on his shoulder. "Come. Let us finish preparations." He casts a glance at Torak and the three communicate something I'm not privy to. We've already done our preparations, so what are they up to, I wonder.

Mirk reaches for my hand, squeezing it lightly. "You are right to miss them. Family—true family—is precious."

Tears mist my eyes. "Beyond precious," I say, my voice a little hoarse as the three of them walk away.

I brush at my eyes and sniff, holding my spine straight as my harem disappears into the crowds.

"Don't tell me you're still crying about home?" a cold voice cuts in from behind me.

I wheel around. Clay. All decked out in purple and gold, from his tunic to the many rings on his fingers. Godhood is really going to his head. He wasn't this overdone on Earth.

"Oh, my poor Lady Lily," Clay snorts and shakes

his head as if in wonder. Then, arrogance flashes over his features. "Don't you see? We're gods now. We have a power that no mortal human can understand."

He holds out his hand and in his palm, a mini monster appears, a black tarantula rearing back on its four legs, but with the head of a snake. Suddenly, it darts forward and hisses, its forked tongue lashing out in my direction.

I can't help myself. I jerk back.

Clay laughs and the illusion evaporates. "Imagine your sisters, faced with that? Are bees akin to the beekeeper? Of course not. That would be ridiculous. Mortals are merely tools. Playthings, even."

It's then that I see his escort, a woman standing a few feet back and to the side. She's pale, with heavy bags under her eyes from weeping, stress, and lack of sleep. On her neck, a fresh purple bruise marks her flesh while another one has started fading on her arm. So, already, Clay is mistreating his servants. That doesn't surprise me. Why it's allowed, *does*. You'd think this place would be a lot more advanced than Earth, considering it's ruled by the supreme and divine. But then, maybe that's the problem. Gods are so out of touch with humanity they see them as insects in the dust.

I hate to admit it, even to myself, but Ladron was

right. Gods should never go to Earth. Not if this is how they view people.

"Hey, Lil, did you hear about the stolen arrows?" Clay asks, his voice casual as if we're back in school and he's talking about a trivial class assignment.

I want to walk off. I can't stand him, and I sure don't like him calling me Lil, but I don't want to give him the satisfaction of knowing he's under my skin.

"Nope, nothing about arrows," I say.

"The Arrows of Plague and Pestilence are missing," he gloats, clearly reveling in having information I don't. "Stolen from Apollo himself, no less. I swear, if a thief tried to take anything of mine, I'd have their head. How—"

A full-throated roar slices the air, drowning Clay out, and I whirl.

Something's panicked the crowd, they're screaming and scattering every which way as beneath my feet, the ground trembles.

A wall of people surges towards me and then parts revealing the cyclops cage, tipped on one side.

It's empty.

A stampede of panicked servants, gods and horses flood my vision as they knock me and Clay off the road just in time to notice the cyclops heading directly towards us. It's wielding a chariot in its hands like a club as it smashes the people and horses in its path, as behind it, a row of guards tries to launch their spears, but they look like ants throwing toothpicks for all the effect they're having.

The cyclops tromps closer, crushing bodies beneath its feet, the crunch of bones a sound I won't soon forget as people cry out in agony.

A body flies through air to land a few feet away, crushed to a pulp and unrecognizable. I can't even tell if it's a man or a woman, but I see the emblem of Clay's house on the bloodied tunic.

Clay stares in horror. His face is pale and he backs away, positioning himself behind me, his eyes locked on what's left of his servant on the ground.

Here we go again, me and Clay, repeating history. Me, staring at the danger. Him, using me as a shield, probably getting ready to push me into harm's way. Anything to save his own selfish hide.

Only this time, I can do something.

"Get back," I yell at the guards trying in vain to stop the mayhem.

No one seems to hear me.

There's just too much noise, chaos, and blood.

One of the guards, taller than the rest and with a

spear that sparkles, launches his weapon at the cyclops' furry legs. The spear bounces off, barely making a scratch.

But the cyclops notices. It pivots and brings the chariot down on the man, smashing him against the stone wall, ripping his body apart.

"Get back," someone else yells.

It's Alfio, his aged voice unexpectedly loud, and as it carries through the chaos, this time, the guards listen.

They pull back, away from harm.

It's my chance. I've got a clear shot. Something inside me stirs, instinct I suppose, but something that rings of experience, as well. I pull my spear off my back and twist it in my hand, letting the weight of it settle into my arm and then I heft it high above my head, set, aim and launch.

The Spear of Truth whistles through the air, straight and true.

And hits its mark, dead center, straight into the cyclops' eye.

The creature screams, a bone-jarring sound and drops the chariot to claw its bleeding face.

It flails, striking out blindly, but there's no one within reach anymore.

A calm seems to settle over it for just a moment, then it sniffs, holding a hand over its eye, and turns and flees, its powerful legs quick, carrying it out through the gates and into the distance, away from the carnage it wrought.

I swallow, a little nauseous at the bodies littering the cobblestones and the coppery scent of blood fouling the air.

"Thank the gods," someone yells.

A ragged cheer breaks out, growing stronger by the second as people ask, "Who was it? Who threw the spear?"

"Who saved us?"

Eyes turn my way just as Clay steps forward and bows.

"Epimetheus!" the crowd begins to cheer.

He lifts his hands and grins at me, soaking up all the attention as the people rush his way, jostling past me to throw accolades at his feet like roses.

"Epimetheus, the Brave Epimetheus has saved us," they begin to chant.

"Yes, it was *my* spear that saved you," he says, raising his voice above the singing. I suppose there is one thing he really is good at. He's such a big bag of hot air, he doesn't have a problem outshouting a crowd. He's so pleased with himself as he adds with that self-important grin, "I could do nothing less than protect my people. I will put myself between you and danger."

I turn away in disgust. In all the chaos, I somehow ended up on the other side of the court-yard, away from the gates. I begin pushing my way back, ready to leave this place—and especially Clay, but along the way, I pass the cyclops' cage.

It's huge, and still on its side. And it's not bent or broken, but looks in perfect condition, as you'd expect a creation of Hephaestus to be. The door is wide open, so it doesn't seem the cage was the problem. But where is the lock?

Around me, the cheering intensifies, and I look up to see Clay being borne away on a litter, followed by an adoring crowd.

I roll my eyes and turn back to the cage, but Alfio is standing there, his expression unusually sharp for such an old face.

"The people may think what they like," he says. "But I saw the truth with my own eyes, my goddess." He bows, and I swear I can almost hear his old bones creak. "Thank you for saving us."

"No problem," I say, reaching over to give him a

helping hand to stand back up. "Any god could have done it."

Alfio flicks a glance at Clay's disappearing litter. "No. Not any god."

That makes me laugh a little, and then thinking back to how he echoed my order, I say, "Your voice seems to carry some weight with the guards. It's a good thing they listened."

Alfio chuckles. "Let's just say that I, too, saved them once or twice. A long time ago." Then, he shakes his head as if in disgust. "The people should know that Epimetheus didn't save them. They're only setting themselves up for hardship when he fails next time."

"Why not tell them yourself?" I ask.

He raises an eyebrow at me. "And why not you?"

I nod, getting his point.

His bent shoulders sag as he sighs. "Fame is a troublesome thing, is it not, goddess? The people love to lift up a hero, only to see them fall."

"Yeah, the world is a crazy place," I say, shaking my head.

Something glitters in the dust near my feet.

The lock.

It lays on the ground, open and in perfect condition.

I stare, and at my side, I hear Alfio's sharp intake of breath.

"The cyclops didn't escape," I say. "Someone set it free."

[11]

"*EVERY HEART SINGS A SONG, incomplete, until another heart whispers back. Those who wish to sing always find a song. At the touch of a lover, everyone becomes a poet.*"
~ *Plato*

"LILY, YOU'RE SAFE!" LADRON'S VOICE IS A CARESS after such violence.

He sprints up to my side with Mirk and Torak close behind, and though he's not out of breath, there's a sense of urgency and worry about him.

"Amazing," Torak says. "The wolves are saying you defeated the cyclops with one throw." He's looking at me with such awe and desire that my heart hiccups in my chest.

"It was the spear," I say, always one to shrug off a compliment. Maybe that's part of the reason others find it so easy to steal credit from me.

"Even more impressive," Mirk insists. "Few can wield that weapon."

"Indeed," Ladron agrees, looking at me with eyes so full of delicious promises that I want to claim all right now.

But now is distinctly not the time for such thoughts.

"Let's get out of here," I say, and if I'm a bit breathless, none of my companions make mention of it. "Looks like a good time with everyone distracted to slip out unnoticed."

I glance down at the lock sprawled before my feet. "Will there be an investigation?" I ask, feeling a bit reluctant to leave when a crime has been committed. "Someone let this creature free. Someone is responsible for all these deaths," I say, looking around at the carnage once again.

Ladron slips an arm around my waist. "I cannot say. Too many politics involved to know precisely. What I do know is you need to leave before they discover this lock."

"Why?" I ask.

Mirk and Torak exchange a knowing look and I

sigh, thoroughly annoyed that I don't share their secret language. Yet.

"That beast was from your land. Your dungeons. If anyone close to Zeus wanted to hurt you, they could plant the seed that you should be held responsible for this," Ladron says.

Clay.

Shit.

"But I just got here. I haven't even seen my land." Even as I say the words, I know the truth. It won't matter. If someone wants me to suffer, they'll find a way. "Guess we better jam then," I say. "Out of sight, out of mind."

Let's just hope that will be true for us.

THE MEN HAVE SUCH LONG LEGS THAT I HAVE TO skip every few steps to keep up, but with the goddess strength flowing through me, it's not a problem.

I spend the beginning of our journey absorbed in the beauty and wonder of my new world as I try to rid my mind of the cyclops attack, of all those mangled bodies, of how good it felt to throw that spear...too many juxtaposed emotions to sort through.

We have about three days of travel ahead of us, and I intend to use this time to acclimate to being a goddess and a queen while learning all I can.

That's what I'm focusing on during this trip.

Yup.

I am definitely *not* thinking about sleeping under the stars by a campfire with three of the sexiest men I've ever met.

Nope.

"Tell me about my queendom," I say, breaking a long silence.

When no one immediately chimes in with an answer, I push. "Come on, guys. There must be something noteworthy about it besides being the hellscape for monsters. What are our exports? What are we famous for?"

"Nothing," Mirk says with a flash of white teeth.

Before I can even interpret his response, he suddenly disappears. Like, literally. There one second, gone the next.

My mouth drops open and I stop in the road, looking to Ladron for some kind of explanation.

"Your kingdom is very poor," he says. "And known solely as the Land of the Dungeons."

I shake my head and wave at the empty air. "Are

we not going to talk about that? Mirk? He just…vanished."

"Ah." Ladron acknowledges with a nod. "He is Hades' son."

I glance at Torak, but he just shrugs.

"Is he gone? Did he teleport?" Then, the brain cells connect. *Right*, invisibility. I glance around, not sure I like having that much smoky sexiness stalking around when I don't know what's there. "So, he has Hades' Helm of Darkness? Have we pissed off Hades, too? Another son stealing treasures from a vault?"

Ladron grins but shakes his head. "Mirk's talents are his own. The divine blood that flows through his veins has merely strengthened his natural fae abilities."

Intrigued, I ask, "What else can he do?"

A dryer smile touches Ladron's lips. "He's not exactly the sharing sort, if you haven't noticed."

That pulls a small smile of my own, but then Mirk reappears a few feet in front of us. "Epimetheus' fleet," he says, pointing ahead between two hills, where I catch a glimpse of the sea dotted with black sails.

Clay's ships. I purse my lips. Hopefully, that'll be the last I see of him. Like, for centuries.

Then, I grin.

There *is* a bright side to my queendom, after all. It's so tiny, remote, and desolate, Clay will never set foot in the place.

And that's the best lemonade anyone can ask for.

"Be careful. Monsters from your worst nightmares run in these parts," Ladron's deep voice slips through the darkness.

I look over to see the outline of his tall, lean body against the twinkling lights of Mount Olympus in the distance. It's late and we've made camp for the night, high in the Greek mountains.

"Just getting some cool water for Alfio," I say. Traveling is hard on his old bones. Torak had to practically carry him from the donkey to the bed we made for him with the sole fur packed in our burlap sack.

"Don't wander far," Ladron calls after me.

I drop my hand on the hilt of my sword as I head for the dark line of trees. As much as I've tried to push the memories aside, I can't help but recall the horror the cyclops inflicted on so many in such a short time. What other monsters might we face while traveling by foot? Was this part of Zeus's plan? To dispose of us by beast attack?

The hairs raise on the back of my neck as I head into the shadows, but then, deep inside, something stirs, a rock-solid inner source of strength that feels like its rolling its eyes with a pffft. My goddess self? I've walked all day, in brand new boots, and I'm still energized. There's so much to explore, to learn, about myself and the world around me. I refuse to let Zeus, monsters, or a shitty queendom ruin my afterlife/new life as a goddess.

The scent of pine hangs heavy in the air as I follow the sounds of the brook, gurgling along the forest floor. There's a fairy-tale beauty surrounding me, dappled moonlight bathing the rocks, trees, and the occasional fleeing woodland creature in a silvery glow.

It's magical. Probably even more so, because I've never really camped before. My parents weren't campers. Their fledging career in that field apparently died on their first trip to Yosemite Valley shortly after Melanie was born. After seeing black bears pop open the trash can next to the tent to eat dirty diapers, my mother refused to ever set foot in a tent again. Nylon is no defense against sharp claws.

Thinking of my mother makes my throat close, and in the darkness, it's not so easy to shove that thought away. I only succeed because I'm still too close to camp to really cry my heart out. For that, I want to be alone. No doubt, once I get to my kingdom, I'll have some time and space to myself where I can face the shadows haunting me.

A glistening brook winds its way through the trees, but I don't stop to fill the waterskin. I'm caught in a spell I don't want to break. The ground dips a little as up ahead the stream widens into a pool nestled at the base of a large outcropping of rock, looking as if some Titan had picked up the side of a mountain and simply dropped it there.

It's an idyllic scene, like one of those Thomas Worthington Whittredge paintings I saw on a fourth-grade school trip to the art museum. I kneel beside the pool and swirl my fingers in the water. It's cool, soothing. The perfect bath after a hot, dusty day.

Grinning in anticipation, I reach for my legging laces.

Something rustles in the undergrowth to my left.

The word 'monsters' snags in my mind, Ladron's warning ringing out as I yank my sword from its sheathe and clutch it tightly as I walk. After a few yards, I pause beneath an ancient pine, sword raised. Where is the blasted thing? The last thing I want to do is run straight into its open arms.

I hold my breath and spin in a slow circle.

Nothing moves.

A small gust of wind brings fresh scents, mint and thyme.

An owl hoots, far in the distance.

Then, a stick snaps near the outcropping of rock. I'm ready to bolt, but when I see Torak stepping into a shaft of moonlight, I freeze.

He stretches, and the moon's silver rays plays over his skin as he unbuckles his harness. The pauldrons drop to the forest floor. The leather-paneled war skirt quickly follows.

I'm frozen in place, my breath caught in my throat as he stands there, magnificently naked, a work of art that puts Michelangelo to shame. Raw power, sinew, muscle.

I see every inch of him—including those well-endowed inches that summons a liquid fire between my thighs. I know I should close my eyes or shuffle away, but I can't seem to move.

I'm caught in a seductive imagining of what it would feel like to have his body pressed against me. Inside me. What would it be like to make love to this delicious man? Nothing like the fumbling, awkward encounters I've experienced before, I know that for certain.

I nibble my bottom lip, my heart picking up speed as an ache, deep inside, begins to build.

Torak turns his head.

I hold my breath.

He faces me, and in the moonlight, his eyes almost seem to glow. Then, he steps back into the shadows, and I realize they really *are* glowing, bright green. And he's looking straight at me. I wince. Of course, he's a wolf, isn't he? Not only can he see me in the dark, he can smell me, too—along with the fact I'm aroused, probably.

I heave a sigh, sheathe my sword, and step out from my hiding place under the tree.

A moment later, he's standing in front of me, still gloriously naked. And closer up, it's even more impossible to avert my gaze. His powerful body is seductive, but it's the man behind the muscles who truly mesmerizes me. As much as my body aches for his, my heart yearns to know his deepest secrets, his darkest truths, and to share my own with him.

"You're comfortable in your skin, aren't you?" I blurt. I never could ignore elephants in rooms. Especially elephants dripping blatant sex appeal.

"And you?" he asks, arching a brow.

"Me?" I almost forget to breathe as his hungry, predatory gaze threatens to devour me. "Naked?"

He grins and, despite the situation, I immediately relax as my lips curve in response. What power does he possess that makes the world so safe a place? When I stand beside him, I *know* I'm not alone. Just as I know I won't be judged as inadequate. He'll be there, a solid comfort through any trial or tribulation destiny throws at me. He'll never run away. He is the personification of loyalty itself...every tantalizing inch of him.

"Are you comfortable in your own skin?" he queries lightly.

I snort. "I'm not so bold as you." I'm not the inhibited type, but I'm also not ready to stand naked in front of someone I've only known a couple of days, either—despite how safe he makes me feel.

He lowers his gaze to my lips and then searches my eyes, and for a moment, I think he's going to kiss me, but instead, he seems to fold into himself. The next second, he's dropping to all fours, and before he hits the ground, he shifts into a magnificent white wolf at least five times the size of a normal one.

I gasp in admiration and watch, stunned, as he bounds away, disappearing into the trees.

I wait three seconds and then exhale, releasing the tension, half relieved he's gone, and half disappointed. I don't worry he's rejected me. I know he hasn't. We have a bond. Somehow. And it's a bond of complete trust.

I return to the pool and splash the water on my face before filling the forgotten waterskin. When I'm done, I twist the cap shut and sit back on my heels, hugging my knees.

If only I could Skype Melanie and Sarah. They'd love Torak. His boldness. His muscles, of course. And most of all, his magical freaking grin that makes it all safe. Melanie would laugh and... My breath catches. I'm never going to hear Melanie laugh again.

The box of thoughts bursts like a dam. Memories flood me, at first so fast and so intense that I can't process anything. But then, I see one of my favorites zooming past and I grab onto it like a lifeguard's red rescue tube and hold tight.

My mother making oatmeal cookies while me and my sisters sit in front of the TV in our matching tiger onesies. I'm excited to be watching Hercules for the hundredth time. Even though my sisters are more interested in the cookies, they love watching the movie with me all the same.

Tears flow. I wipe them with the back of my hand. Who knew that experience would prove the first step on a path that led me here? Cut off from my sisters forever. If only I could see them again. Just once. To let them know I'm fine. That I didn't really suffer, and that I am, in fact, enjoying myself, surrounded by gorgeous, sexy men.

The tears keep coming so hard that I can't wipe them away fast enough. Giving up, I just let them fall in hot rivers down my cheeks. I weep, my shoulders shaking with the depth of my pain.

I don't hear him when he returns. I only feel his warm nose, nuzzling my hand, and when I look up, I see the mighty white wolf has stalked to my side. I throw my arms about his neck and bury my face in his soft, silky fur. And I just let the pain consume me.

He stays by my side, a pillar of strength, as I sob until I hiccup, and then hysterically sob some more.

And still he doesn't move, even after the sobs slowly subside.

Finally, my body empties itself of the last tear, at least for now. I sit in silence. Exhausted. Only when a cloud covers the moon do I wonder how long we've been here. I sit up and glance back through the trees. The campfire will be nothing but a dull orange glow by now, if not ash.

"Thanks," I whisper, threading my fingers through Torak's fur.

He turns his head and places his cheek softly against mine. He stays there, letting me know that

I'm his. He's mine. Then, and only then, does he bound away, vanishing back into the woods.

I'm nearly back at the camp when I hear him, the mournful howl of a wolf who is so much more, and I know, deep in my soul, he truly shares my grief.

"MUSIC IS A MORAL LAW. It gives soul to the universe, wings to the mind, flight to the imagination, and charm and gaiety to life and to everything." ~ Plato

A FAMILIAR SOUND WELCOMES ME AS I NEAR OUR campfire. Ladron sits on a log, flames dancing against his flawless skin, as he strums his lyre.

The music seems to rise like a wave from the delicate instrument. I can almost see the notes as vibrant colors swaying against the night sky.

I sit across from him, my gaze locked on his full lips as he begins to sing.

He glows with the magic he's creating with his music, his voice ethereal and seducing.

I think of the day I woke in his presence, his music pulling me into consciousness. I should have known then that he was Hermes. It was so obvious, thinking back.

Still lost in the dance of Ladron's music, I glance around the fire.

Mirk is nowhere to be seen, but that doesn't mean he's not around.

Alfio is already tucked into the furs, snoring loudly. It tugs at the memory of my dad, and rather than shove it back into a box, I let it wash over me and away. At least for now. Ladron's music helps me do that, helps me find a healthy balance for my emotions. A middle ground between losing my shit and bottling up my shit.

Eventually, I scoot closer, and twine my arm through Ladron's as he plays, laying my head on his shoulder. He looks down at me as he sings, directing his words—his magic—straight to me, and I absorb the spell of his breath, his voice, his melodic tenor, letting it fill me.

It's as intimate as a kiss—more so even. It is another kind of union altogether, to feel his magic inside me.

Torak slips into camp much later, and Ladron places his lyre back into his case as we settle into sleep. Torak stays in wolf form and rests at my feet, keeping them warm with his fur. It's my first night with all three of them, and there's a feeling of completion as I stare at the splattering of bright stars in the sky while I listen to each of them breathing. Mirk takes the spot to my left and Ladron to my right, so with a small movement, I can touch any or all of them to assure myself they are here, with me. That I'm not alone in this bizarre Alice in Wonderland adventure.

I sleep well that night. Deeply and without dreams.

BY LATE AFTERNOON THE NEXT DAY, WE'RE ON the side of another rocky mountain as the sun beats down on us without mercy. It's the kind of heat that makes even talking a Herculean task. I mentally pause at my own comparison and realize…I'm in the world where Hercules lives. These aren't just expressions anymore. They're real!

Mind blown, I think of as many expressions and sayings which had originated from Greek Myth as I can muster. Sour grapes (from Aesop's fable). Beware of Greeks bearing gifts (from the Trojan horse), the

Midas Touch (King Midas's wish from Dionysus)... there are so many.

This mental list goes on for some time. We continue to walk as Alfio clops along on his donkey, each of us lost in our own thoughts. As the heat bears down on me mercilessly, my thoughts turn from Greek linguistic influence and leaking Dungeons to Iced Caramel Macchiatos and Bubble Tea in air-conditioned cafés.

Last summer, I spent every Saturday studying at Bobalicious, a tiny hole-in-the-wall café where I camped out with my books, sipping Thai Milk Tea with an extra serving of tapioca pearls. That is, until Sarah and Melanie tracked me down. With me leaving so soon for college, we wanted to cram in as many memories as we could, watching movies, hanging out... If only I'd spent more time with them...

I grimace, and as my heart hurts again, I fall to the back of the party where Torak leads Alfio on the donkey.

"If only the donkey knew a wolf holds the reins," I tease, relaxing already. Somehow, Torak's presence alone makes my pain a little less raw.

"He knows." The corner of his lip lifts in a smile. "It's why he's behaving."

I grin in response. He's as much a pillar of comfort now as he was last night, massive paws anchored to the ground in the silent statement he's there to stay. The thought makes me feel a cozy warmth inside, but that warmth turns into a different kind of heat as I drop an appreciative gaze over his muscled abs. He seems allergic to wearing shirts. I've yet to see one on him, and I am definitely not complaining.

I turn my attention to Alfio. He's looking weaker by the hour, and I'm worried the journey is too much for him.

"Are you remembering to drink water, Alfio?" I ask.

"This heat, 'tisn't natural," he grumbles, but reaches for the waterskin.

"Yeah, it ranks right up there with Death Valley —" I begin when Torak interrupts me with a low whistle.

He comes to a stop. "A fitting name," he murmurs, his eyes locked ahead.

I follow the line of his gaze to where Ladron stands on a shelf of rock overlooking the valley below, and as I join him, I see the desolation, the miles of rocky, dry terrain, fanning in all directions that promises nothing but heat and more heat.

Then, I see why Torak whistled. Directly below, the river runs through a grove of great oaks, but they're dead, sticking up from the ground like twisted, rotten carrots. And from here, the water looks almost black.

"Something has killed the trees," Ladron says when I give him a worried glance.

My gut already knows the answer, but I ask anyway, "Is the water flowing from my kingdom?"

His lips thin in a silent 'yes' that renews my sense of urgency.

"Let's go," I say, turning back to the road.

"We should tread with care," Ladron warns, staying me with a hand. "I've seen such devastation before, centuries ago. The rot left behind stemmed from the foul breath and blood of a hydra."

My hand drops instinctively to my whip.

"It was, indeed, a hydra," Mirk suddenly appears, stepping out of thin air.

"Whoa," I gasp, stumbling back a little, but he's quick to catch my elbow in a steady hand.

"Forgive me," he murmurs. For a second, a gleam flashes in his eye, one that makes me keenly aware of the warmth of his fingers through the soft leather of my sleeve, but then, it vanishes, and his expression turns grim. "I've just returned from scouting ahead. It's been at least a fortnight since the attack. The dryads, unfortunately…did not survive."

His words make me sick to my stomach. I hadn't considered the trees being inhabited.

"And the hydra?" Ladron asks.

"Gone," Mirk replies. "The route ahead is safe. For now."

"Then, let's hurry before that changes," I say, stepping back onto the road.

Ladron and Mirk join me, but Torak…he doesn't. He stands still, facing the decimated grove, his face stoic, his hands fisted tightly, a twitch in his clenched jaw his only emotional tell.

I slip over to him and place my palm on his back. He jerks, startled by the contact, which shows just how lost in thought he is. No one ever sneaks up on the man with wolf instincts.

"What is it?" I ask softly. Clearly something is deeply troubling him.

"I knew them," he says, his voice deadly quiet.

Oh god. "The dryads?"

He nods once, sharply. "They cared for me one summer…after I was badly injured. They offered me shelter and protection until I was strong enough to move on."

Torak turns his head to look at me, his eyes reflecting the pain he's holding so tightly in his heart.

I reach for his hand, gently opening his fist until I can slip my fingers through his. "I'm so sorry." I almost ask if he's sure this is the right place, but of course he wouldn't make a mistake like that.

He turns to Mirk. "Are you positive there were no survivors?" he asks.

Mirk's face softens, his normal smirk wiped away as genuine compassion reflects in his eyes instead. "There were none. My deepest sympathies."

"I must see for myself," Torak says, shifting into a wolf and running forward, towards the grove.

Those of us remaining quicken our pace, following the path of Torak, but still, the sun is nearly set by the time we reach the valley floor. Above, dark clouds gather, and a wind begins to blow.

While I welcome the coolness it brings, the creaking of the dead branches around me is an ominous one. The trees are much bigger close up, their height and girth telling me they once stood green and tall over the river weaving its way through their spreading roots. But now, they're black, their trunks scorched with acid. And the souls within will never walk here again.

We push forward, surveying the damage in

silence, but as we reach the end of the grove, I close my eyes to whisper a prayer and a promise, "May you rest in peace, and may no more of your kind suffer such a fate on my kingdom's behalf. I shall stop this. I swear it."

Torak approaches one tree in particular, lifts his wolf chin to the sky and howls with so much pain and heartache it nearly breaks me. Tears run down my cheeks, spilling onto the ruined soil at my feet. Mirk and Ladron bow their heads in respect.

After some time, Torak shifts back into his human form and approaches us, the grief on his face now replaced by rage. "We must hunt. We must find the hydra that did this and slaughter it."

Mirk nods. "I'm with the wolf," he says with a slight look of disdain that he and Torak agree on something. "I may not have had the personal relationship Torak did with this grove...but as a fae I have a connection to these lands and the dryad that demands I seek justice for this slaughter."

Ladron shakes his head. "We cannot rush into this with such haste. As tragic as this is, we have other urgent matters to consider. Like getting to the Dungeons and finding a way to keep the rest of the monsters from escaping and wreaking even more havoc."

I'm not surprised Torak wants to avenge his friends, nor that Mirk is angling for a fight. I too feel a feral urge to hunt and kill the beast that did this. I can feel the emptiness of the trees in a way I've never known before, and it's a crushing feeling, like all the warmth has been sucked away, leaving a bone-chilling coldness behind. Still, I hesitate, and I realize this might be my first truly queenly decision. Do we hunt the hydra and stop one monster, or keep on our journey and stop many more?

They all look to me for an answer, and I hate to hurt Torak with my decision, especially when I don't really know if I'm choosing correctly.

"I'm sorry," I say, my gaze settling on Torak's. "But Ladron is right. There will be more deaths, more destruction, if we don't get to my queendom quickly. The hydra could be anywhere by now with a two-week head start."

Ladron nods encouragingly and Mirk doesn't look too upset over my decision, but a flash of pain crosses Torak's face and I cringe. Already the weight of my crown feels too heavy, and I haven't even arrived at my queendom.

A pall settles over us as we leave the trees behind, and with each step I'm even more determined to find

Prometheus to fix this mess. I will scour the Dungeons myself if that's what it takes.

When we've finally left the trees behind us, I turn to Ladron. "Where is it safe to stop in these lands?" I'm strong enough to travel all night, but I know Alfio and the donkey can't. Still, I want to get as far from the devastated grove as I can.

"There's a village, Oia, about two hours away." Ladron points to the south. "On the edge of the Stone Forest."

I glance back at Alfio and the donkey, and then up at the dark clouds churning overhead. "Let's hurry," I say. "It looks like rain."

IT'S BEEN RAINING STEADILY FOR THE PAST HOUR, and I'm anxious to get Alfio under a roof before he gets sick, but the first glimpse of Oia makes us all pause. It even brings Mirk back into his visible state once again.

"'Tisn't natural," Alfio is the first to say what we're all thinking.

"Do they always keep the village this dark?" I ask.

There's not a single light visible from the small cluster of stone buildings ahead, but with all the rain, it's hard to be sure. Or so I tell myself. I don't want to think about the alternative right now.

"I'll look," Torak volunteers, handing me the donkey's reins. It's the first time he's spoken since my decision, and I know he's taking time to process his grief.

He takes off for the village but out of courtesy to the donkey, doesn't shift into his wolf form until he's a good thirty feet away. The donkey stamps his back hoof anyway, but he leaves his disapproval at that. He's too tired to bray.

We wait, trying to shelter Alfio from the storm while listening to the rain drumming against the stones and rocks around us. I know I'm safe with Mirk and Ladron alert and wary by my side, but after the cyclops attack, then the hydra destruction, I'm on guard, my hand frequently falling to the whip at my hip.

Torak bounds out of the darkness, transitioning into his human form in one fluid, graceful leap.

"The village is abandoned," he announces, shaking the water from his long hair. "There's no one left and no trace of friend or foe. I'd guess whatever happened here isn't recent. A month ago, maybe more, judging from the lack of scent." He tilts his head towards Alfio huddled on the donkey's back.

"But there is shelter, and we should take advantage of it."

Goosebumps prickle my skin. I'm not all that keen on staying in someone else's deserted home, but I know Alfio has reached his limit. He can't keep traveling without some kind of rest, even if it weren't for the rain. Still, I'm uncomfortable as I agree, "Alright. Let's do it."

We head into the village, cautious, watchful, and as I follow Torak's lead, I catch glimpses of the buildings around me in the flashes of the lightning arcing through the sky. Yes, the village is empty, but it still has a story to tell. The occasional basket dropped in a doorway. A soggy blanket draped over a window. A child's shoe.

"They left in haste," Ladron comments at my side.

"Did monsters from the Dungeons chase them away?" I ask, shivering.

No one answers.

They don't have to.

Torak takes us to the inn, the largest building at the edge of the village with a receiving hall and two small guest rooms off to the side. As Ladron starts a fire in the center pit, I help Alfio to a bed and rummage around for dry blankets.

"I'll make sure you get something to eat," I promise as I swath him in a virtual cocoon.

"Thank you, m'lady," the old man replies, managing a feeble smile.

He looks so frail it makes me frown in alarm, and I'm still frowning when I return to Ladron's now crackling fire.

"Just one more day before we get to my kingdom, right?" I ask, pensive.

"Alfio is tough," Ladron replies softly, easily reading the heart of my concern. He points to several bottles on a nearby table. "I found wine, and Mirk will return soon with food. Both will do him good."

And they do. Less than two hours later, Alfio is snoring comfortably in his bed, and I'm lounging on a cushion, cupping a mug of warm wine with my feet toasting nicely by the fire.

Outside, the rain still rages, but inside, Ladron is seated across the fire from me, playing the lyre, his elegant fingers dancing over the strings. Mirk lounges by the door, arms folded behind his head, ankles crossed, his body a contradiction as he somehow manages to simultaneously relax and stay on the alert. He reminds me of a cat, committed to his nap but ready to pounce at a moment's notice. And Torak, in his massive wolf form, lays stretched out on the floor, eyes closed, ears upright. We haven't talked about the hydra, but he grazed my finger with his during our walk here, and his lips lifted into the smallest smile, which briefly gives me some peace. It's been only a couple of days, but I feel a connection to these men that will not be easily severed.

Slowly, my lashes drop over my eyes and I deepen myself into the cushions, letting the warmth and the music seep into my bones.

I don't even notice I've fallen asleep until it's the next morning and the sun kisses my skin.

"Let me give you a hand, Alfio," I hear Torak's deep voice in the room nearby. "It's time to rise. The bathhouse is warm and waiting."

The idea of a bath sounds like heaven, but I'm not about to take a real one here. Not in a mysteriously deserted village.

I yawn, stretch, and rise.

The others have already gone.

After grabbing a linen towel from the pile someone has placed on a nearby table, I head outside in search of water.

The sky is blue, and already, it's warm enough to make me miss the rain from the night before. It's going to be another hot day, but at least, tonight, I'll be in my own kingdom. I can't call it home yet. The thought of calling anything but the Lemon cottage 'home' feels just wrong.

I find the cistern to the left of the inn. It's fairly large, like your average water garden, and it even has a small stone bridge spanning its length. There's about six inches of water at the bottom, and it's cool against my skin as I lean down to wet my towel.

I straddle the bridge and drop the damp towel over my face when I hear the thud behind me.

"Hello?" I ask, my words muffled by the cloth.

I expect one of the men to answer, but when I only hear what sounds like a shower of rocks, I whip the towel from my face and jerk around.

I frown. I'm alone. "Hello?" I lift myself to my feet. "Mirk? Is that you?"

I hold my breath and listen.

Nothing. There's nothing here. No birds. Not even the buzz of a fly. I shiver, suddenly wanting to dash back inside the inn like I'm ten years old again, tearing through the darkness each time after mom made me take out the trash at night.

Yeah, I'm outta here.

But I take only three steps before I hear a deep, rumbling growl.

My heart skips a beat.

And it's only then I think to look up.

A giant creature crouches on the roof. Two giant, black, bat like wings sprout from its shoulder blades. Its massive body the tawny gold of a lion, but the shaggy mane surrounds a humanoid head instead of a big cat's. And the tail is nothing of the feline variety but that of a scorpion, laced with poisonous barbs.

I stare, my feet rooted to the spot.

The creature's eyes narrow and it dips its head to open its mouth wide, displaying rows of sharp, pointed teeth.

I remember what it is then: a manticore. Incredibly deadly, dangerous, and according to all the books I've read, a creature that is not only impossible to beat, but one that can kill a god.

And...I've left my weapons inside. The only thing I've got to defend myself is a wet linen towel.

My finger twitches.

The creature locks in on the movement immediately and crouches as if to spring.

But before I can move, there's a new growl and a flash of white fur leaps across my field of vision.

It's Torak.

The manticore screams and jumps straight at me, claws extended just as Torak leaps. His massive white paws catch me in a protective embrace and together, we roll on the ground as the manticore swoops low, its massive wings sending huge downdrafts of air. It's a near miss, and with a keening cry, it launches itself into the sky and flies away.

I draw a shaky breath.

The wolf beneath me stirs and then turns into a man.

"There is little mystery left here," Torak says, his eyes flashing. "Of course, they were fleeing a flying beast. A creature from the sky leaves little scent on the ground. I'm such a fool."

"No," I say, my voice wobbling. Torak's anything but a fool. He makes me feel safe, warm, wrapped in the ultimate bear—or I guess wolf—hug. And I can't move. I just lay on top of him, my fingers welded to the leather straps of his harness. Yeah, I'm never letting him go. He's my anchor, and right now, I need something solid. Immovable.

He looks at me, his expression vulnerable. "You were right. If we'd gone after the hydra, more monsters would have escaped. You'll be a great queen, Lily Lemon," he says softly, his lips barely an inch from mine.

His pure maleness is overwhelming, and I welcome the chance to be swept away, away from the reality of a world filled with monsters.

His eyes are so beautiful, so green. And the way

his hair spills over his broad muscled shoulders as I lay on his chest makes me want to run my hands over every inch of his skin.

I don't think, don't question myself. I erase that last inch between us, pressing my mouth to his, partly out of relief I'm still alive and not in the claws of a manticore, and partly because he's so damn sexy, so loyal, and he just feels right.

He kisses me back, crushing me against him with strong, muscular arms, his mouth hot as his tongue explores mine. He moans into my mouth and I feel his arousal press against my belly, which spreads the heat from our mouths all the way down my body.

His hands lower to cup my ass, pulling me in closer against him.

But then he pauses, pulling his mouth from mine.

"As much as I would really love to see where this goes, we've got to leave before that manticore comes back."

I ease out of his arms, shivering at the loss, but knowing he's right.

By the time we find the others, my heartrate has returned to normal, but my lips still feel deliciously swollen as we hit the road, less than a day's walk to my future.

The terrain changes with every hour we travel.

The rugged shards of rock protrude higher from the ground, until finally, they stand in tall limestone formations, forming a virtual wall that marches up a steep hill and disappears over the horizon.

"Your kingdom lies on the other side of that hill," Ladron says, training his gaze ahead.

My heart begins to pound.

I'm here. Beneath my feet are the Dungeons. Prometheus. I climb the hill, my heart beating faster until finally, I reach the top and look out over my kingdom.

Mountains hem a flat, rolling plain on all sides but the west. The sea covers that border. And the soil is gray. As far as I can see, there's not even a single weed. How bad does it have to be when even weeds give up trying to grow?

It's a land so desolate that even I, Lily Lemon, fear it'll be impossible to make lemonade out of this batch of particularly rotten, moldy lemons.

[13]

"THOSE WHO INTEND on becoming great should love neither themselves nor their own things, but only what is just, whether it happens to be done by themselves or others." ~ Plato

"I SHOULD HAVE STUDIED FARM MANAGEMENT OR Environmental Engineering instead of Greek Classics," I say, grimly surveying the bleak landscape spreading out before me.

Ladron arches an elegantly confused brow.

But I don't explain. I squint at the walled city in the distance, tucked in the shadow of a single mountain rising up from the plains. Two craggy, massive towers of rock jut out from the mountain's side to stand like sentinels. On top of one pillar a white stone palace sprawls, and on the other, a temple. The surrounding fields are dry, barren, and in some, the soil is black.

"Why is the soil dying?" I ask. "Are the Dungeons at fault?"

Mirk blinks into existence by my side to say, "Only Prometheus knows."

For now, maybe. I lift my chin. These people are about to see some genuine Lemon determination. "Just where are these Dungeons, anyway?"

Ladron points to the twin towers of rock. "The Dungeon entrance lies there, at Charakas, your ruling city. Between those two cliffs."

I survey them grimly. Shit's about to get real.

I set off down the road toward my city. Normally, I'd feel strange thinking about a city as 'mine,' but on this journey, the crown has settled more, and I find myself with a powerful drive to protect my land and my people. To set things right. From a distance, the hundreds of stone-tiled roofs glistening from within the walls look tidy and inviting, like one of those medieval towns on a travel brochure. But the closer I get, the more I see crumbling walls, chipping plasters, and cracking tiles. The village is just sad, a ruin of what it once was.

"This place… 'tisn't natural," Alfio mutters on the donkey.

"It isn't," I agree, as a piece of my heart seals itself to the struggling people of my queendom. "How can anyone survive?"

No one answers because it's obvious no one *can* survive in such a place.

The sight that greets me at the city gates leaves a hollow pain in my gut. The people are lined on either side of the road, but it's clear by their solemn faces they would rather be somewhere—anywhere—else. They're thin, grim, dirty, reminding me of the black and white photos I've seen of the 1930s Pennsylvania coalminers. And in their eyes, they have that same look of hopelessness, too.

Ladron steps in front of me and raises his hand. "Citizens of Charakas," he addresses them. "Welcome your queen. Lily, Queen of the Dungeons."

A woman steps out of the crowd. She's young, not much older than me, and she has the most startling eyes—a piercing blue that sweep over me, pinning me with their judgement, as if I swung on the scales of justice. Her white-blonde hair is cropped in a short pixie cut, but she's no delicate, frail flower type. She's powerful, commanding. Her silver loop earrings match the inlaid bracers on her muscular arms. The leather strip vest she's wearing over a short red tunic is sculpted to her body and is scuffed, worn with use.

She nods once, as if she's made up her mind about me and, as every eye in crowd locks onto her, she executes a slow, respectful bow.

I exhale a silent breath of relief.

"My lady, I am Hailey, Blacksmith of Charakas," she says, her strong voice carrying easily over the men and women gathered here. "Allow me to welcome you to your town."

She gives the citizens lining the streets a pointed look, and they follow her example to bow, but with obvious reluctance. One man, bald, built like a bull and with a jagged scar on his cheek, is the last to bend. There's anger storming in his eyes, but under that, I can't miss he looks as haunted as the rest. It's clear they've all suffered here.

Hailey faces me once again and I step forward, every version of any welcome speech I imagined instantly evaporating from my mind.

"Thank you—" I begin.

A rotten pomegranate cuts me short, splatting on the road at my feet.

Hailey whirls to the right, and in three strides, she's reaching into the crowd as Ladron and Mirk draw themselves to their full height.

I step in front of them. These are my people. My kingdom.

"This is not the way, Cy." Hailey yanks out a young boy from behind the angry man with the scarred cheek.

He hangs there like a frightened rabbit. He's thin, scrawny, and looks like the classic street urchin down to the holes in the threadbare knees and elbows of his ragged attire.

"This is your queen," Hailey raises her voice with authority. "You will show her respect. You are better than this."

She lets him go and the boy obediently drops to his knees. As she circles, directing a stern eye to the citizens on the street, the kid leaps to his feet, and the crowd opens to swallow him, taking care of their own.

There's resentment on every face looking at me, but I get it. To them, I'm a drain on already tight resources, just another burden they have to carry as they struggle to survive this bleak world. What use do they have for a queen? And if I'm honest, I'm thinking the same thing, experiencing my moment of doubt over what can I, Lily Lemon, fresh from Earth, actually do for them? Powering through is my only option—that, and honesty.

"I'm going to work hard for you," I promise from the bottom of my heart. "I'll find ways to restore this land. And before you know it, the fields and orchards will be green once again."

The faces watching me are stoic, hardened. Hopeless.

Still, I forge ahead. "Come and tell me your problems. We'll find answers. We will rebuild this place. Together." My speech is short and corny, like something straight out of a cheesy novel, maybe not even that good, but I meant every word of it. Lemon's honor.

In the silence that follows, Hailey bows again. "We are most honored and grateful, my queen. Please, allow me to escort you to your palace."

"Thank you," I say.

I follow Hailey through the gates and into the city, keenly aware of every gaze lined on that street tracking each of my steps.

Ladron keeps close by my side, and Mirk remains visible as he stalks a few paces behind. Torak, as always, brings up the rear, leading Alfio on the donkey.

"How long has it been like this?" I ask Hailey, skipping a few steps to join her at the front. "The gray soil? The state of the village?" I wave at the buildings.

There's not one that doesn't have broken tiles. Several have actual holes in the stone walls, as if they'd been struck by a cannon, or more likely, I suppose, a lightning bolt.

"These lands have always been harsh and unforgiving, but the past twenty or so years have been brutal," Hailey answers, leading me past a rundown apothecary shop and up a steep road zigzagging to the palace above. "Every spring, more land dies. We have little left, only our goats and sheep. And now, these past few weeks, we stand in danger of losing even them. I fear we are cursed."

I thin my lips. Maybe we are, considering the run of bad luck I've had myself lately. "Your livestock? What's happening?"

"It's a mystery." Hailey gives a puzzled frown. "They're vanishing, my lady. Gone in the night with no trace. The scent hounds have yet to find a trail."

"No trail?" That's familiar. I glance at Ladron, and I can see he's already thinking what I am. Manticore. Village, Part Two. "Have you heard any news from Oia?" I ask Hailey. "Survivors, maybe?"

"Survivors?" She stops in the road, her blue eyes suffusing with horror. "What disaster has befallen them?"

I bite my lip. Not the way to break news, Lily.

What if she had family there? But I'm already knee-deep in my mistake, so I continue, "The village is empty. It looks like everyone fled. And when we left this morning, we were attacked by a manticore."

Her eyes widen and she continues walking, more quickly now. "Manticores haven't been seen in hundreds of years."

Well, with the Dungeons open, you're about to see that and a lot more, I want to say, but I don't. I've already dumped enough bad news on her right as is. Instead, I swear, "I'll find the creature and stop this."

Yes, the creature is strong—capable of killing a god—but there are four of us against one. Right? Hailey looks skeptical and Ladron's frowning, but my mind is already buzzing with plans. I need to find the leaks in the Dungeons and figure out a way to patch them, even temporarily, while we search for Prometheus. After getting killed by the hellhounds, facing off with a cyclops, and seeing the devastation wrought by a hydra, I'm not messing around. Queen Lily is about to kick ass and take names. Mostly by being very well organized.

When we arrive at the top, I get a closer look at the buildings covering each cliff. To the right, the temple stands on its own mesa, isolated from the main landmass and accessible only by crossing an arched stone bridge. To the left, my palace takes up every inch of flat land and a lot that isn't. The foundation is carved directly into the limestone itself, and there's not even space for the tiniest of gardens. The few trees I see cling desperately to the palace walls, hanging precariously over a breathtaking plunge to the valley floor below.

And that valley floor is what captures my attention most, because I know, between the bottom of these two cliffs lies the entrance to the Dungeons. To Prometheus. To the answers of all these problems.

"Your servants await your pleasure, my queen," Hailey waves me toward an entrance flanked with clusters of terra-cotta pots filled with scraggly fig trees and faded pink flowers. "This way."

I follow, surveying my new home. The word makes me wince. It's hard to even think that word applies here. Home is the Lemon Cottage, with Melanie, Sarah, and my mom and dad. Not some Greek palace built into a mountain overlooking the entrance to Dungeons filled with genuine monsters.

I step into an inner courtyard where a handful of servants are lined up under an olive tree. The tree stands out. It's the only healthy-looking member of the plant kingdom I've seen the entire day.

"This is Cora, your mistress of servants," Hailey introduces the woman at the head of the line.

Cora is a middle-aged, freckled redhead with a serviceable dress that hangs off her gaunt frame like a hanger. "Pleased to serve you, my queen." She bows low, then rises to ask, "How may I serve you, my queen?" And then bows again.

Already, the bows and the 'my queens' are getting old, but I decide to save that conversation for another time. Right now, Alfio looks like he's going to drop. I turn him over to Cora's care and then follow Hailey into the palace for a tour.

It's huge. About the size of a shopping mall and without the convenient Shopper Directories on each floor. But it's gorgeous, everything a Greek palace should be, and according to Hailey, built by Prometheus himself. I'm led through room after room of tiled frescos, tall, stately columns, and wide windows that offer sweeping—albeit dismal—views of my kingdom. I suppose, once, they framed fertile fields and green trees, but now, there is only dry, dying soil fanning out in all directions.

Somewhere during the tour, I lose Ladron and Torak. As for Mirk, he's either reverted to invisibility or he left with the others. I follow Hailey, but when I'm shown yet another room, what looks like a library of scrolls this time, I realize I'm exhausted and have had enough. It's the scrolls that tip me off. Lily Lemon, the Greek Classic student, would have jumped and squealed with joy at the sight of all those tightly rolled, stacked manuscripts holding who knew what secrets. But the Lily I am right now is too preoccupied with the Dungeons along with her kingdoms safety and well-being to even think about reading.

"Thank you, I've seen so much I'm worried I'll forget it all," I tell Hailey. "I've kept you long enough. I really don't want to be a burden."

Hailey gives me a smile and another bow. "Rest well, my lady. If you have need of me, send word to my forge."

When she leaves, I wander back through the spacious corridors and down to the feasting hall. The pool that runs through the center is filled with clear water that magnifies the intricate tilework of dolphins and crabs lining the bottom.

"My lady, we have brought food and wine."

I look up to see Cora and two young girls bearing platters of fruit, bread, nuts, and coriander fish.

I join them as they place the food on a small table next to a white silk draped couch and then quickly vanish from the chamber, leaving Cora alone.

"It looks so delicious," I tell her, admiring the

apples carved into swans. "And I thank you for the courtesy, Cora, but how can I eat this when you have so little? Please, take this and share it amongst yourselves." I look up into her astonished eyes as I add, "I am a goddess. Food is solely a pleasure for me."

"My queen…" she begins hesitantly.

"I insist," I say, stepping back. "Please, deliver it to those most in need." I'd deliver the food to them myself, but after my greeting at the gates, I'm sure the people aren't all that thrilled to see me right now.

"As you wish." She takes the fish but can't carry more as she hurries from the room.

It's then I see Torak entering from the opposite side.

"This place is so huge, we're going to need cellphones," I say.

He cocks a brow, but he doesn't ask. I guess he's getting used to my strange comments now and then. I watch him walk my way, his muscled thighs flexing under the panels of his war skirt. It's impossible not to admire the long, lean lines of his body.

"Is Alfio resting?" I ask, when he comes to a stop before me. "I want to make sure he's well cared for."

"Shouldn't he be caring for *you?*" Torak teases lightly, amusement flickering deep in his green eyes.

I smile. "*Tisn't natural.*"

He laughs and I stare up at him, his closeness reminding me of the past times we stood this way, how the moonlight fell on his face, his naked body. How he stayed by my side. And... of course, his lips. I step closer, thinking of his kiss, and I can tell he is, too.

His head begins to drop.

There's a soft scuffle behind me and I glance back to see Cora has returned for the remaining food.

"My queen," she murmurs.

When I turn back to Torak, he's stepping away from me. "I'll check on Alfio," he volunteers with a grin.

I release a breath, and as he leaves the feasting hall, I do, too.

I wander through the palace, and eventually, I find myself leaning against another window, looking out over my kingdom as the sun sets. There's no wrapping a bow over this one. There's no lemonade. It's a shitty place. And it's now my home. The knowledge weighs me down, like the Dungeons beneath are trying to pull me into their dark, grimy depths.

It hits home, then.

And I sob. Gut-wrenching sobs.

This is it. I live in a luxurious palace now, but I'd give the world to spend just one more night in the homey cottage of my childhood, filled with warmth and love. I miss them all, I even miss the cluttered messes and the bickering. Sarah, leaving her shoes in the middle of the room and Melanie, griping she's always having to clean up after her younger sisters.

I miss them. I know with time, the pain will ease, but it will never go away, no matter how long the centuries drag.

I wipe the tears with the back of my hand. The palace is dark, silent as a tomb—and just as drafty. In the long hallway ahead, the dull orange glow of fire-light dances shadows against the stone wall. As I round a corner, I'm faced with a long, marble staircase leading into a spacious living area below. The entire side is bathed in warm firelight, and as I step foot on the top stair, something dark flies across the stones.

I gasp and duck as the shadow turns into a soaring eagle and flies across the wall.

Shadow puppets.

I blink and hold still as a flower blooms.

Slowly, I sit down on the steps, watching as birds fly. Flowers grow. Fish swim past, and then, all manner of Greek things: hydras, centaurs, and pythons.

There's beauty here. Hope.

Curious as to who is working this magic, I silently

steal down the stairs and turn. Mirk stands there, waiting for me and holding my gaze steadily with his. He says nothing, but his silver eyes take in my red-rimmed ones, the tears drying on my cheeks. He brushes his thumb against my chin as he passes.

I watch him go. He's as unique as Torak. As Ladron. I need each one of them, in more ways than one.

I head back up the stairs and fall into the first bed I can find.

Tomorrow, it's time to start solving the big problems.

Tomorrow, I will figure out how to save my kingdom.

Tonight, I need some damn sleep.

14

"YOU WILL NEVER DO anything in this world without courage. It is the greatest quality of the mind next to honor." ~Aristotle

THE SOUND OF LADRON'S LYRE THRUMS SOFTLY through the air as I adjust my grip on my whip while stalking around the olive tree, looking for a target. It's early, and the sun struggles to break through an overcast sky.

"There are only so many places a manticore can hide here," I say, cracking the whip to slice a shriveled olive suspended from the branch above. It falls on the courtyard stones with a soft plop. "There's only this mountain and the Dungeons beneath."

Ladron's music stops.

I look over to see him watching me with a small, concerned smile that makes me suspect he's going all protective. It's thoughtful, of course, and I know he's being that way because I'm a freshly minted goddess, but I'm ready to hold my own. I may not know who I am, but my soul is remembering how to be a goddess.

"If the manticore sneaks back to hide in the Dungeons, then I'll solve two problems at once," I tell him. "The manticore and the Dungeon leak."

He shifts his long legs. "We should move with care," he cautions. "This isn't an ordinary monster. Its tail venom is fatal even to the divine, *Lilyitsa*. It's dangerous."

"As is letting it free to prance around and treat my kingdom like an all-you-can-eat buffet," I say. "I'm not letting that happen, so we're tracking this thing down today and getting rid of it."

Ladron reads my determination and, after a moment, defers to me with a nod. "Most likely, such a creature would take to the caves," he says, setting his lyre down to rise to his feet. "We should start there."

I grin and begin circling the tree again. "The others should be here soon," I say, plucking another withered olive with the tip of my whip.

As the olive falls, Mirk steps out of the air just in

time to catch it neatly in his outstretched palm. His lip quirks in a half smile as he locks a sensual gaze with mine. This time, I don't look away. Beneath all that scorching charisma, there's a soul of a poet which makes his intensity more comfortable. More mine. And this morning, he's particularly fun to admire rocking a leather vest with a crimson cravat tied around his neck, a fae thing, I suppose, and one that is definitely working for him.

My heart speeds up a notch, and then I hear the scuffle of boots behind and I turn to see Torak striding into the courtyard, offering a dazzling display of muscles that provides another distraction.

"You called?" Torak asks with a yawn that makes me smile. True to his wolf form, he's a late riser, preferring to run long into the night with the moon. Getting up this early must be killing him.

"Yes, I called," I answer, looping my whip back through my belt and straightening my shoulders to face all three of them. "We're hunting down this manticore, before it eats all the livestock and renders us as devastated as the Village of Oia.

Ladron nods thoughtfully, but he's no longer objecting.

Mirk doesn't react, and that makes me think he

was there eavesdropping the entire time. He and I might need to have a talk about spying at some point.

As for Torak? His lip is curled back in a grin that gives me a momentary glimpse of the wolf he is beneath. "Then let us hunt," he says. I know at least part of his enthusiasm stems from my orders to leave the hydra. He needs something to punish for the death of his friends.

We leave immediately, heading out through the gates and down the road. The temple on the opposite cliff looks sinister in the dim lighting. I squint, noting for the first time that the damage is more extensive than I'd originally thought. When we turn a bend in the path, a grove of scraggly pines block my view, but I make a mental note to ask Hailey about it.

By the time we get to the village below, the gray sky is filled with lightening, with shafts of gold and pink breaking through. The streets are quiet, with only a few people moving about. By far the loudest sound is our own booted feet striking the cobblestones.

We're nearly at the main gates when I hear the shouts.

I break into a run and sprint around the apothecary shop to see Hailey standing before Cy. The youngster is clearly distraught and still wearing the same tattered clothes from the day before.

A group of grim looking men surround them, some armed with axes, a few with pitchforks, and two with swords. Fear of an impending attack flashes across my thoughts, but when I look closer I can see the worry and compassion in their eyes. They're alert, guarded, and listening.

Hailey looks up as we arrive, her dark brows drawn in a concerned scowl.

"What happened?" I ask.

"It's Elias," she says, giving the boy's scrawny shoulder a comforting squeeze. "His father. You were right, it's a manticore."

Cy looks up at me, his brown eyes are round, solemn circles and his tears leave white trails down his grimy cheeks. "The monster took him," he croaks, his bottom lip trembling. "We stayed all night with the sheep. A-and at dawn, the m-monster…it just came out of the sky. It…" he chokes and makes a swooping motion with his hand that tells me he saw the creature carry his dad off.

I flinch. I'm too late. Another attack. And this time, a person lost instead of a sheep. "I'm sorry," I whisper, reaching over to give the boy's shoulder a squeeze myself. "We'll search for him. I promise." I want to promise the kid the world, that we'll find his father safe and healthy and bring him back. But I've been lied to by grownups before...by my sperm donor...and it's never a better option for the child involved. Still, I make him a silent vow in my heart that I will do everything I can to bring his dad back to him. Alive. And if there's a chance of that, I need to move now.

I turn to Hailey and I can see she's thinking the same thing. "We're heading out," she says, her leather armor creaking as she hoists a double axe over her shoulder. The beautifully crafted weapon is huge and must weigh a ton. I can only imagine the strength it takes to work with metal and fire all day.

"It's got to be the same manticore we encountered on the way here," I say in a low voice as we step away from Cy. "Are there any deep caverns in this area? Something big enough for such a creature to hide?"

"Two." She nods. "West, around the mountain at the base near the Dungeon Gates, and to the east, there's another set, near the hot springs."

"Then let's divide and conquer," I say. "I'll take west." It's time I saw these mighty gates to my Dungeons, anyway. Maybe the caverns are the leak. "Safe hunting."

As Hailey and the gathered men head east, I

wave for Ladron, Torak, and Mirk to follow and set off at a run. The fear we're already too late lends an extra urgency, and I run faster than I ever have before.

I skirt the city walls, heading for the Dungeon Gates between the cliffs as Torak shifts into his wolf form and bounds ahead to scout. The terrain is uneven, rocky, and what trees there are have few leaves.

I spot the Dungeon gates from a distance, but am still awed by the enormity of them.

They're impressive. Massive. The outline of two doors are carved straight into the mountainside, reaching at least one hundred feet tall in classic, over-sized Greek style. But that thought makes me pause. Maybe they're not oversized, after all. Maybe there's a monster that big lurking inside, a monster I'll encounter when I search for Prometheus. When I think about the variety of monsters that exist in the myths and legends, I shudder. That's what I'll be facing within the Dungeons. And that's what this world—and Earth—will be facing if I don't stop them.

"They don't look breached," I say, as Mirk and Ladron come to a stop by my side. "And I don't see caves."

"The gates are untouched," Ladron says. "Zeus' seal still holds."

Torak switches back to human form while standing at the base of the cliff, almost directly under the temple above.

We sprint over to join him and there, behind a jagged outcropping of rock, is a large cavern with a wide mouth. Large blue-tinged crystals hang down from the ceiling, and rock and dislodged stones litter the floor. In the dark recesses are several gaping holes, leading deeper into the mountain.

"Let's go," I say.

We draw our weapons and head inside, but the exploration is a short one. There's nothing here. The caves are shallow, each ending against a sheer wall of rock within fifteen feet.

I'm disappointed and worried as we withdraw from the last one. "Perhaps Hailey had better luck," I say. It's pretty unlikely the manticore has kept Elias alive this long, but I can only cross my fingers and hope.

We take off, running at speeds so fast that to the naked eye, I'm sure we're just a blur, and it's not that long before we're meeting Hailey's party coming down from the mountain's side.

There's no sign of Elias.

Hailey frowns. "Nothing."

I nod. "Same."

I draw a deep breath. There's a lot of mountain left, and every passing moment only seals Elias' fate. *Think, Lily. Don't crack under pressure like a squishy lemon.*

After a few moments, the puzzle pieces click together, and I know I'm right as I point to the cliffs above me. "We're in the wrong place. The manticore was on the roof in the village, watching from high in broad daylight."

Hailey's brows rise. "The temple's dangerously unstable. It's unsafe to pass."

"Sounds like the perfect manticore hiding place," I say, and a good candidate for a breach. "Onward," I say, feeling like a hero on an adventure, only my heart is beating too fast and my nerves are on edge with fear.

We sprint so fast, the local men with us can't keep up. But we don't wait. We leave them behind. Every second is precious.

Minutes later, we're standing at the foot of the bridge spanning the gap between the mountainside and the temple complex. Even damaged, the temple itself looks solid, but I can only stare at the bridge with amazement at how it has yet to collapse. It's a skeleton, hung together by a fragile hope. That's it. Not even a prayer remains.

"I'll go first," Ladron says, taking a step forward.

"Don't be silly," I say, stopping him with a raised hand. "It's me. I'm smaller than all of you."

"It's dangerous," the protective side of Ladron comes out again. "This bridge is unstable, Lily—"

I cut him short. "I've made up my mind."

Yeah, it's dangerous, but at the thought of one of my people over there, possibly still alive, I shove all other concerns aside and step onto the bridge.

On Earth, I never was one for heights. Even walking on the second floor of a shopping mall gave me the willies. But now, I'm not bothered so much, even when I see through the holes at my feet and down the dizzying depths to the treetops below. It's a fall and then some, but I've got this.

I'm halfway over when the stones gives out from under me and begin to vibrate. Shit. I'm off like a rocket, leaping over the gaps before me as the entire structure wobbles.

Behind me, I hear the shouts of warning and fear, then the sound of rock against rock. I don't have far to go, but the stones beneath me are now gyrating back and forth so far, I'm losing my balance. I grab my whip and crack the leather coil, curling it around the end posts, now just a few feet away.

The whip catches, and I jump, just as the stones vanish beneath my feet.

As I roll forward, my shoulder hits the hard dirt. The ground beneath me shakes and I hear the heavy, dull rumble of stone striking the mountainside only to drop down into the valley below.

I leap to my feet and twist around.

Ladron's hanging from the post at the far end of the bridge. Below him, on a ledge about fifty feet under, a white wolf is laying on its side, motionless.

"No!" I gasp.

"Help," a voice moans behind me. "Help me. Please."

I draw my sword and whirl in one smooth motion. Behind a column to my right, I see boots.

I spare a glance at Torak, still lying prone on the ledge, but there's nothing I can do beyond reminding myself he's a god. He's tough. He's not that easy to kill. And right now, I just might have found Elias. I've got to focus. I sprint toward the feet.

It's a man sprawled out on the ground, and he's injured. Blood seeps from a cut on his bald head and there's deep claw marks along his back, but he's alive. This must be Elias. The joy I feel is somewhat damped by my concerns for Torak as I drop to my knees by the man's side.

"Elias?"

He nods.

"Can you stand?" I ask, glancing at the stone structures above me. The manticore has to be here, somewhere. "We've got to get out of this place." Somehow. Or hide before it comes back.

Elias moans, and it takes some doing, but after a few tries, I manage to get him to his feet. He's dazed, confused, and unsteady, leaning on me heavily with each step. It's clear we're not going anywhere fast.

A flash of gold glints from the corner of my eye and my heart sinks. The manticore, like it was just waiting for me to be in the worst possible position before it attacks. I turn, and sure enough, there, on the tiles, the manticore crouches, its massive paws twitching back and forth as it readies itself to spring.

Running is out of the question. I'm stuck on this mesa until I find an alternate way down, or someone sends a Pegasus to the rescue or something.

"Hide, Elias," I hiss, pushing him toward an outbuilding about fifteen yards away. As he staggers forward, I brandish my sword. "Looks like we're doing this," I yell at the manticore, trying to draw its attention from Elias.

The beast flicks its ears and glares at me from under half-closed eyes. It really does have a creepy face, like it's part human, part demon maybe. It looks disgusted, maybe even a little insulted that I would think myself capable of distracting it so simply. Clearly I've underestimated its intelligence. I blink. Just how smart *is* this thing?

Suddenly, it springs.

I barely manage to roll away as it launches itself over me and swipes at my chest with its massive paws.

Its claws strike the column above me, scoring the stone deeply. I swallow. If its claws can slice through stone like butter, they can damage my god-like flesh just as easily. And just how severely injured does a god have to be to die here? Prometheus got his liver removed daily for centuries. Tantalus condemned to an eternity of hunger and thirst. If this creature is considered a god-killer...I'm not sure I want to know what it's capable of.

As it arcs in the air to shoot itself toward me, I scramble to my feet and leap after Elias.

"Run," I shout, pulling him behind me as I dive toward the building.

He's weak and stumbles, but I drag him forward.

The manticore roars behind me, and I know its

divebombing me again, but I focus on the door ahead instead.

Ten feet. Six feet.

I'm almost there.

Then, I'm shoving Elias through the threshold as the stench of sulfur blasts my nostrils.

I dive after him, but something burns my arm.

Then there is a great thud as a venomous spike embeds itself deep into the stone near me. I look down and see I'm bleeding—but it's not red as I expected. It's gold. I'm not made of blood anymore, I realize. I'm made of ichor. The shimmering under-tones mesmerize me until the manticore roars, reminding me of the stakes. It's only a few feet away.

"Keep going," I shout at Elias, who moves forward abruptly and nearly trips.

At his feet is a crack in the ground, a misshaped hole that wreaks of sulfur.

"Jump," I shout.

But when he doesn't move, I don't give him the choice. I tackle him from behind and together, we fall into the breach.

15

"Suffering becomes beautiful when anyone bears great calamities with cheerfulness, not through insensibility but through greatness of mind." –Aristotle

My stomach drops as I plunge into the darkness, and it's a long enough descent that I have time to worry Elias will break his neck. My sword clangs, bouncing off the rock walls around me as I manage to twist midair, just enough to protect Elias by hitting the ground first. The impact shocks every bone, joint, and tendon in my body, and even though I land first, the fall still knocks the air out of Elias on top of me.

"Are you okay?" I ask, the coppery scent of his

blood mixes with the sulfur around me as I roll him off and onto the rocky, cavern floor.

Elias drags a shuddering breath, but manages to nod as I help him sit up, and then I'm on my feet, astonished at how fast I'm recovering. This fall would have shattered every bone in my old Earthly body, but as a goddess, I just feel a vague sense of bruising that's already fading. This inspires hope in me on behalf of Torak, but also brings my attention back to my still bleeding and burning arm. The fact neither has stopped tells me all I need to know. I've got to get out of these Dungeons and fast, before the god-killing venom Ladron warned me about takes over and finishes its job.

"What are you doing?" Elias asks at the sound of tearing cloth.

I look up while ripping a strip from the bottom of my shirt. "Hoping Girl Scout First Aid works on goddesses," I say. Technically, I know I'm supposed to hold still so the venom doesn't spread, but that's obviously not an option. Instead, I settle for wrapping my arm as tightly as I can to staunch the flow of ichor. It's a struggle with one hand and I'm a bit distracted by the fact that I'm bleeding gold. It's such a trip to see this magical ooze coming out of my body.

As I tie the last loop of the bandage with the aid

of my mouth, I scan the area for my sword. It's dim, the shaft of light falling from above the only source of light, but it's enough to illuminate the metal jammed into the rocks about five yards away.

I sprint over the piles of bones and curled rams' horns littering the floor and I'm just closing my hand over the hilt when a shower of rocks falls from above and the sound of the manticore's sniffing grunts echo down.

Shit. It'll figure out where we went if it hasn't already.

I run back to Elias and yank him to his feet.

"We've got to move," I hiss, but my tongue feels strangely numb in my mouth and my words come out more like, "We gahh thoo moo." I wince. In no way is this good, but I don't have time to worry right now.

Another avalanche of gravel falls from above.

Elias tries to walk, but he's moving too slow. I grab his arm, loop it around my neck, and pull him after me.

"I can't," he pants. "Leave me here."

I want to tell him I won't, because I promised his son that I'd do everything I could to bring him home alive, and that I'd never leave any of my people behind. But I can't navigate that many syllables right now, so I settle for a grunt as I drag him forward.

The loudness of a roar from above tells me the manticore is poking his head down the hole and has likely spotted us. I don't look. I run. Straight for the tunnels opening in front of me.

I have a split second to make a choice, so I mentally cross my fingers for luck and choose the tunnel that seems to be heading down.

A cascade of falling rocks and roars reverberate in the cavern behind me, telegraphing the location of the manticore and its rapid approach.

"I can't," Elias sobs as I manhandle him into the tunnel.

This time, I don't even bother grunting. I'm beginning to sweat, and it takes all of my concentration to rush headlong with him into the dark.

It's as black as pitch and every few yards, my feet fall through thin air before they hit the solid ground I expect. It's stomach turning, but I have no choice but to run down the steep incline at full speed and as blind as a bat.

The manticore's roars mix with Elias' sobs as we continue our mad descent. At odd intervals, something sticky brushes against my face. Spider webs? The thought kicks me into berserker mode, and despite the fact I can't swallow and every inch of skin on my body is now burning, I charge down the tunnel at breakneck speed.

My head pounds.

Reality distorts, like I'm underwater. Sound and light bend in strange ways and the world tilts and spins around me.

Still, I run. Instinct propels me even as sweat burns my eyes and blurs what remains of my vision. I stay focused on the light ahead, real or imagined, it's what keeps me going, keeps me pulling Elias, his weight that of the dead, though he still, fortunately, breathes.

I am finally close enough to see where the light emerges. There's a crack, a small one, in the wall up ahead. Barely big enough for us to squeeze through. I sway on my feet, nearly losing grip of Elias, my palm slick with sweat.

The manticore snorts in the distance behind me, the sound of pounding feet shaking the tunnels.

Panicking, I stumble to the wall and shove Elias out first, and it's not until I see his leg vanish that my slow thinking catches up with me. What if I've just shoved him off the cliff?

Something bites my leg and I know it doesn't

matter. Staying would only get us eaten alive. I dive through the crack after him.

The light is so blinding I close my eyes in pain. The air is fresh, there's no sulfur here, but then, the burning I've been fighting flashes over my entire body. I fall to my knees, my heart sinking with the knowledge I can't battle this venom any longer. It's too strong.

I try to stand, to open my eyes, but my body refuses to obey.

There's nothing I can do but fall into the darkness that's rising to swallow me whole.

MY EYELIDS PEEL OPEN LIKE SANDPAPER. MIRK IS wrapping his crimson cravat around my arm. When he notices me looking at him, he glances up. There's fear in his eyes, and his brows are drawn in a troubled line. "Don't move, Lily. Stay still. We've got to stop the venom."

He didn't have to worry. I couldn't move if I tried. My skin is so hot, and my body feels like lead, including my eyelids, so I close them again.

Everything fades.

When it comes back, it's all disjointed. I get

glimpses of Mirk carrying me down a steep mountainside, my cheek bumps against his leather-clad chest as he slides on the rocks.

Then, Ladron's hovering over me, his eyes filled with concern. "You're going to be fine, *Lilyitsa*," he says.

I surrender to the darkness again and awaken to the sound of a donkey braying. But my consciousness is short lived. Why is it so hard to keep my eyes open?

Voices flitter in and out of my consciousness. Ladron's music, the soft growl of Torak. Mirk's soothing whispers.

When I come to, I'm lying in a bed with soft, silk sheets smooth against my skin—skin that's no longer burning.

"Take another drink," a woman says. Hailey?

A gentle hand slips beneath my head and something cool is pressed against my lips. The liquid is refreshing, tasting of honey, lemons, and flowers, and with each swallow, I feel strength returning, but my head is throbbing at the base of my skull. I'm just not ready to open my eyes.

"Good job," Hailey says as I drain the last drop. She guides my head back to the pillow. "Get some more rest now."

Keeping my eyes closed, I burrow back into bed with relief that I don't have to get up yet.

"'Tisn't fair she was hurt," Alfio's voice grumbles from somewhere near the foot of the bed.

"She'll be fine. She's growing stronger by the hour," Hailey assures.

But each word she says sounds farther and farther away as I let myself drift back to sleep.

The next time consciousness returns for good. I yawn and stretch, but it takes a few seconds to recognize my surroundings and the memories start trickling back.

The manticore. Elias.. My palace…

Right. I'm in my palace, and in a room that's an oasis of comfort despite the stark reality of my kingdom. Painted dolphins frolic on the walls near the ceiling. A fire pit burns low in the center of the room, even though the three arched windows are open and it seems like a warm afternoon outside judging by the bright blue sky.

The bed I'm on is covered in silk and furs, and gauzy curtains fall all around me from a ring on the ceiling.

On a nearby couch, my gaze snags on the long, crimson scarf on top of my neatly folded clothing. Mirk's scarf. He'd tied it on my arm... I glance down and flex my muscles. There's no pain and not even a scar. I'm as good as new. How? And what else am I forgetting? Something's hovering on the edge of my mind—

A knock on the door cuts through my thoughts.

"You're awake. Good. It'll be easier to get you to drink this, then." Hailey grins as she enters my room with an amber glass of golden liquid. She looks like anything but a nurse with her bronze-studded leather vest and her sword swinging from her belt.

"Thank you," I say as she hands me the glass of liquid. It smells incredible, all honey and flowers. "Thanks for taking care of me."

"My pleasure." She points to the elixir. "Bottom's up." As I drink, she drags a chair closer and props her boots on the foot of the bed. "The tavern minstrels already sing songs of you," she says with a conversational grin.

I swallow the last drop and wipe my mouth. As far as medicine goes, this one tastes heavenly. "Good ones, I hope."

"It's all *little goddess Lily slays the mighty manticore. She's a hero,*" she drawls and gives her lip a wry twist.

"But I didn't slay the manticore," I say. "I just ran from it, and…" Suddenly, the memory hanging on the edge of my mind flashes before my eyes. The white wolf, lying motionless on the ledge of rock. "*Torak?*" I sit up in alarm.

Hailey removes her feet from the bed and reaches over to pat my arm. "Torak's fine. Broke his back, but there's no need to fret. He's practically as good as new now, been lying in bed this past week, same as you."

"His back?" I shudder at the thought. That must have hurt like hell. Then, I realize what she said. "I've been out a week?"

"Amazing, really, that you've recovered this fast." She shrugs as she settles back and gets comfortable again. "Manticore venom has killed stronger gods than you."

"I didn't get a full dose."

Hailey snorts. "It doesn't take one."

"Then if I'm alive, it's thanks to you, obviously," I say as I hand her the cup. "And whatever is in here."

"One of Circe's healing potions," Hailey says, absently beginning to toss the cup from hand to hand. Her eyes take on a faraway look that seems almost angry. "That's what my father wanted me to study. Medicine. He's still convinced a woman can't become a decent blacksmith."

"Who's your father?" I ask, curious about her life. "Anyone I'd know?"

It's such a strange question to ask someone, but I

don't know how else to frame it until I remember my past here.

Her jaw twitches. "Hephaestus."

My jaw drops. "Like, *the* Hephaestus?"

She nods. "It's very hard to prove the god of blacksmithing wrong."

Her eyes flick back to mine and she gives me an apologetic, lopsided grin. "Never mind. It all worked out this time. You don't need to hear about my silly family drama."

I swing my legs out of bed and face her. "They aren't silly, and I hope to talk more with you. I could use a friend here."

A smile lights up her eyes. "You got it."

"How's Elias?" I ask, belatedly remembering the whole point of the mission. He'd been pretty injured.

"He's fine, too, but he'll take longer to heal. Another week or so. Can't say he'll be too pleased to hear what the minstrels are singing about him, though." She gives a dry laugh.

"Well, I didn't slay the manticore," I say, recalling her previous words. "I've been out a week? Hasn't it come back?"

"Not since Ladron and Mirk temporarily sealed the cracks," she tells me, rising to her feet in a creak of leather. "Looks like their makeshift plan is working, at least for now."

"It wouldn't hurt you to rest a bit more," she says as I walk to the window, my mind full of the things I neglected doing while I was unconscious. I've wasted precious time that could have been used mapping the Dungeons and trying to find Prometheus.

"I'm resting," I say. "I'm just sick of that bed." There's a smaller room connecting to this one and through the wide doorway, I see a table cluttered with cosmetic jars and a polished bronze mirror on the wall. And, Holy Blessed Lemons, "A *bathtub*."

Hailey chuckles. "I'll have hot water sent up," she says, hooking her thumb over her shoulder. "I'll check on you later, then."

I just grin.

An hour later, I'm finally stepping out of the luxury that is hot steaming water. A few fizzy bath bombs would have made it perfect, but how you get baking soda and citric acid here is a mystery. If my kingdom wasn't on the verge of ruin with a vicious monster at its door, I'd be tempted to start the first pizzeria, espresso, bed and bath business.

I wrap myself in soft, linen toweling and head back to the bedroom. Someone placed a blue gown on the bed, and I slowly ease it over my shoulders, letting the silk glide across my skin.

As I slip my feet into a pair of soft, leather sandals, my eye again catches on Mirk's crimson scarf. Images of his shadow puppets collide with the fear I'd seen in his dark eyes as he'd tied the scarf on my arm. I trail a fingertip down the long line of silk. Mirk's an interesting man, and a smoking hot, sensual one.

Letting my thoughts rove over his complexities, I absently retie his scarf around my arm. It feels personal, a bit like I'm wearing his sweatshirt, and I like it. With a final tug adjusting the bow, I wheel around and head for the door.

It's time I check on Torak.

16

"Music is the movement of sound to reach the soul for the education of its virtue." ~ Plato

I STEP INTO TORAK'S ROOM TO FIND HIM sprawled on his bed, looking devastatingly sexy with sleep-tousled hair. He's as shirtless as ever, and even in bed, he's wearing a war-skirt.

"You're up and about. How are you feeling?" he asks, propping himself on an elbow.

I grin. "I'm great. What about you? Hailey said you broke your back?" Even as I say it, I can't stop from flinching and recalling the image of him in wolf form, lying on that mountain. "It's my fault—"

"Nonsense," he shakes his head and rises from the

bed. "I should have saved you." The muscle in his jaw clenches.

I lift my head. "I'm a goddess. I don't need saving. And anyway, I'm fine, now. That's all that counts. But you? Should you be sitting up?"

His eyes flicker with what looks like respect, and then he laughs a little. "I'm fine. I've had broken bones before."

That makes me laugh, too. Considering I'd met him during a tavern brawl, I have no doubt he's telling the truth. "You're a bit of a rabble rouser, aren't you?" I tease.

I lean forward to give his abs a playful punch, but the instant his fingers close over my wrist, I know it's a mistake. There's too much chemistry between us to fool around like that.

I look up into his emerald eyes. He wants me. That's obvious. And I want him, too.

So...why am I twisting free of his grasp and stepping back?

"Well, I was just checking up on you," I say as I head towards the door. "You should rest. We can talk more later."

He doesn't follow, which makes me equal parts hurt and relieved. But by the time I get back to my room, I'm kicking myself for leaving. I stand in the center of my suite, unsure what to do next. Should I go back? I want to—

Hands slide around my waist, cutting off my thoughts. Torak's hands.

I sigh and lean back against muscles as firm as a stone wall. He holds me close, and for a few blissful moments, we stay that way, the only two in the world.

"How did you get in here?" I whisper. "And so quickly? Quietly?"

"Have you ever heard a wolf in the forest?" His breath is hot against my neck.

"No," I murmur.

"Precisely," he says. Then, his lips close over my neck.

I shiver and turn in his arms.

His kiss is demanding, stealing my breath as his mouth plunders mine in a bold search for pleasure, and something far deeper. It's as if he's seeking the essence of my soul. The loyal wolf. A mate for life.

The beast inside me responds, and I kiss him back, our tongues entwining, teasing, and finally, melding with a fire that ignites a storm of desire.

As I press closer against him, he surprises me by tearing his mouth from mine. "I've brought you a gift." His voice rumbles like a growl in his massive chest.

I'm aroused, breathing fast, and the last thing I want is to stop for a gift, but I like watching the way his muscles move as he crosses to the door. Even though I only left him in his room minutes ago, he's changed into a different war-skirt, this one with topaz encrusted leather panels that show tantalizing glimpses of his massive thighs with each step.

As he picks up a bundle of leather from the floor, I admire the line of his chiseled body. He turns, and keeping his green eyes locked with mine, slowly unrolls the bundle to reveal a war-skirt, a harness, and a set of pauldrons. Small. My sized.

"I asked Hailey to make these," he says. His voice turns low, suggestive, "Perhaps you'd care to try them on?"

My breath hitches. I lower my lashes in a 'yes.'

"It is my honor to assist you, my lady," he rumbles low as he steps close behind me.

I lean against his solid chest and shut my eyes. His hands run down, outlining my hips and my thighs as he begins to slowly pull at the silk until he catches the hem and slowly lifts the gown over my head.

My every inch is bare to his eyes. Yet, as always,

with him, I feel so natural, so comfortable. Accepted in all ways. He's all around me and I breathe deeply, inhaling his scent. The heat from his massive body rolls over mine as he reaches around to place the pauldrons on my shoulders first. The harness comes next. He drags the straps across my skin, inch by inch like a lover's tongue to slowly crisscross the leather beneath my breasts. Then, his lips return to my neck and his hands are finally where I want them, on my breasts, kneading. Teasing.

I moan, feeling myself growing even wetter. He's aroused, too. His hard length presses against me through his paneled war-skirt.

"Take me," I whisper, arching against him.

"You've yet to don your gift," he whispers, taking my earlobe into his mouth as he continues to squeeze my breasts.

When he pinches my nipples, I decide I'm done. War-skirts can wait. I turn and, grabbing his harness, pull him back with me onto the bed. He rolls with me onto the feather mattress and pins me beneath him. He leans over me to trail kisses across my bare stomach.

"Torak," I breathe, running my hands over his shoulders, twirling my fingers in his braids.

He works his way up my body, inch by delicious

inch, and when the heat of his mouth covers my breast, I cry out. I'm impatient. I want him. But he takes his time, teasing one nipple and then the other, driving me to a distraction and keeping me more than ready.

I fumble with the laces of his war-skirt and finally untie them. A few seconds later, there's nothing between us.

I dig my nails into his skin and arch. I can feel him against me, hot. Ready.

"I knew you were mine the moment I first saw you," he whispers, letting out a growl of desire.

"That first day?" I moan.

"A wolf mates for life," he whispers, nibbling my ear.

This time, it's me who growls. "Then take me, Torak, *please.*"

He enters me at once. He's huge, and its intense, in the best possible way. I grip his forearms, taking him as he stretches me until at last, I feel his every blissful inch.

His green eyes lock with mine, the expression in them making me feel like the most beautiful woman in the world.

He begins to thrust, slowly at first but with an increasing speed.

I wrap my legs around his hips and my hands rove over his body, reveling in the feel of his smooth skin over the ridges of taut muscle. His mouth claims mine again, greedily this time as our hips rock together, faster and faster as he thrusts deep inside me.

My body begins to tingle, and with one last gasp, my orgasm sweeps me away.

As the last wave of pleasure subsides, Torak utters a low, ragged moan. I lift my hips, taking all of him as he closes his eyes and shudders in his release.

He bites my neck gently as his great shoulders relax and then, he rolls over to my side as we both lay there, damp with sweat, breathing heavily. He gathers me in a tight embrace and kisses me, slow and sweet.

I close my eyes and savor his scent, his heat, his very heartbeat.

But when I lift my lashes once again, it's evening and I realize I fell asleep, naked and draped over Torak's bare chest. He's already awake and absently toying with my hair, winding it around his finger.

When he sees me looking at him, he slips out from under me and after dropping a quick, heated kiss on my mouth, shifts into his wolf form and bounds from the room.

Of course, his wolf is calling. I slide from the bed

and pad over to the windows. There's a full moon hanging in a sky bright with stars.

Less than a minute later, I hear him howling, but it's not a mournful sound this time. It's a full-throated symphony that makes me smile.

Instinct tells me the meaning of that howl; it's a wolf's mating song.

17

"THE GREATEST WAY TO live with honor in this world is to be what we pretend to be." ~ Socrates

I'M UP WITH THE SUN. WHEN I DON'T SEE TORAK asleep next to me, I feel a stab of disappointment, but it's a small one. He's a wolf, born to howl with the moon, and at the thought of last night's serenade, his announcement to the world he found his mate, I can't help but grin.

It's probably a good thing he's not here. I'd only be tempted to spend the entire day in bed, and I really don't have time for that. I'm a goddess with a withering kingdom to run, a destructive manticore to catch, and a trapped Prometheus to find.

Still, my mind wanders back to the previous night as I bathe and choose my clothing for the day. I've just buckled my last boot strap when Mirk's crimson scarf catches my eye. He looked so worried, staring down at me after I escaped the Dungeons. I twirl the scarf in a spiral, letting the swirls draw my thoughts into a deeper trance.

It turns out Mirk is surprisingly sensitive for a son of Hades, but not, I guess, for a fae.

"Should you be up and about, my lady?" There's genuine concern in Cora's voice when I stride through the kitchen door.

She stands at the table, her hands sticky with the dough she's kneading.

Alfio's in the corner, shelling a basket of peas. When he looks up to see me, a smile lights his aged face. "M'lady," he begins, struggling to stand. "'Tis a great thing to see you hale and hearty, at last."

"Don't get up. I'm fine, really, I am." I smile, waving him back to his seat as I turn to Cora. "Never been better." She doesn't believe me, but she smiles all the same. "Have you seen Ladron and the others?"

"They left early this morning, m'lady," Alfio answers in her place. "They've been sealing the Dungeons. But every time they fix up a hole, something escapes through days later. It's a patchwork at best, not a permanent solution. Simple metal and earth won't hold these monsters back. The walls were made with something only Prometheus understands."

The Dungeons. I'm disappointed their attempts to fix the leaks haven't worked, and I'll have to start mapping them immediately so I can find Prometheus sooner rather than later. For that, I need equipment. Starting with some kind of Greek flashlight or something. Even from what little I saw of them, those Dungeons were dark.

I turn back to Cora. "Can you tell me how to get to Hailey's forge?"

She frowns. "Leaving the palace so soon?"

"I'm fine, really," I say, feeling suddenly like I'm back at home, trying desperately to convince my mom to let me go out with my friends after a bout with the flu.

"I'll go with her, Cora."

I turn as a young woman with large, warm brown eyes and a dusting of freckles over her nose steps into the kitchen. Behind her, I see a half dozen young girls. The instant I make eye contact, they all drop into awkward curtseys.

"They keep coming in from the city," Cora says in slightly exasperated tones. "All of them wanting to serve you, my lady. Since the day you brought Elias off that mountain."

"Any updates on him?" I ask.

"He grows stronger by the day, my lady." The new woman says. She hesitates and then adds shyly, "Thanks to you."

When I recall how reckless I was, I shudder. But when the choice is between reckless and dead, I'll pick reckless every time. "We're all lucky," I say. When she and Cora both make noises to object, I just give them a wry shrug and turn to Alfio. "Take care of yourself," I say. "Maybe if you have time you can see what kind of shape our soldiers are in, if we have any at all."

Alfio's eyes twinkle. "And why would ya be thinking I know anything about that?" he asks.

I wink at him. "Let's just say I think there's more to you than you let on."

Alfio huffs and I smile and turn to the new woman. "If you're still willing to escort me, I'd be grateful."

I follow her outside to the courtyard, and as we pass the olive tree, Mirk appears at my side, adjusting his long, lanky legs to match my stride. He's so close I can smell him, soap and sage, and there's a look in his eyes that makes whatever I was going to say fly straight out of my mind.

I hold still.

"This," Mirk murmurs, catching the end of his scarf tied to my arm. He looks at me from under hooded eyes. "With the fae, wearing the scarf of another has a meaning," he says, his voice low, seductive.

He's radiating such raw sensuality the meaning is easy to guess. My heart begins to hammer, and I can't stop myself from leaning closer and looking up at him through lowered lashes of my own. Were all fae so naturally seductive? Or just the ones with those bad boy Hades genes?

Our gazes still locked, I murmur, "I think I'll keep it on." I lift my palm to his chest.

He gives the scarf a tug and his chiseled lips quirk as he whispers, "Oh, you're not ready for me yet."

Then, he's gone, vanishing right under my fingers, and I deflate a little, like he stole the oxygen as he left. But I didn't miss the promise in his voice. I shiver in anticipation as I head towards the gate where my escort is waiting a polite distance away.

She leads me down the hill and across the city. This time, when I encounter the citizens I'm greeted with a quick bow or curtsey. And there's not a hint of resentment on their faces. My step quickens with a budding sense of hope that I can actually gain my people's full respect one day. After they see how hard I'll work on their behalf.

We arrive at Hailey's shop near the village center. Two small bitter almond trees grow in pots outside the front door. Inside, her shop looks more like a warehouse-sized art studio, but with the kind of weapons her father built, I suppose she, like him, is really more an artist than anything else.

Six bellows surround a massive forge, but there's not a speck of ash anywhere to be seen, and on the wall hang paintings of various gods. Zeus with his thunderbolts. Poseidon with his trident. There's even a full-length painting of Prometheus, chained to the rock with ravens on his stomach, ready to dine. The painting gives me pause. He'd done so much for humanity before. I was going to need his help to do it again.

"I keep these paintings here as a reminder," Hailey says, stepping up to my side. "Of the kind of black-smith that I'll never become."

"I get it," I say. "If only weapons didn't have to be made." I turn to her. "We don't make weapons here, do we?"

"On occasion, swords only for defense," she replies. "Living in the shadow of the Dungeons, we must be prepared."

I grimace. "Maybe someday we'll make it safe here again and they won't be needed." It's a pipe dream, but everything starts in a dream, doesn't it? "I came to ask for cave exploration climbing equipment. A lantern, hammer, bolts, whatever I'll need to map the Dungeons."

She waves me through the forge and into an adjoining room. It's quaint, simple, a fireplace with two chairs placed between a golden statue of a lion.

As I sit, the lion shifts to inspect me. Of course. It's imbued with life as Hephaestus is famous for.

"My favorite of dad's cats," Hailey explains, reaching over to scratch the statue behind its ear. It purrs and then settles down to sleep at my feet.

"Amazing," I say. "Truly."

I glance over at her. "Do you mind my asking… are you the daughter of Aphrodite then? Hephaestus —your dad—was married to her, before she died?"

"They were married, yes, but I am not her daughter." She sighs and takes a seat across from me. "My father forged me from metal and used his magic to bring me to life."

My eyes widen and I know shock is written all over my face. "Seriously? So those stories are true? Of gods making kids out of…everything? Zeus' brain even?"

She nods. "Yes, that is true as well."

"Did you come to life as an adult?"

"Yes, but I have had a childhood," she says, leaning forward. "I'm like you, Lily. I died in my god life and lived a human one until I died there and was reincarnated here again. So I know what you're going through, if you ever need…a friend."

She says the word carefully, like she doesn't use it often, and I wonder if she does have any friends in this strange world.

Well, she does now.

I lean over and pull her into a hug. She freezes, surprised, then slowly wraps her arms around me and tightens the embrace.

Emotion clogs my throat as I sniff and pull away. I had no idea how much I needed to talk to someone who knows what I'm going through until she said that.

"Thank you," I say. "I needed this." But I can see I've lost her attention. She's staring down at my boots, an odd expression on her face. "What is it?" I ask.

"Let me…" she murmurs and then crouches beside me to swipe a finger on the buckle of my boots. Rising slowly, she squints. "Interesting."

I lean forward. There's an orange, glittery dust on

her finger. "Is that a bad interesting or a good interesting?"

"It might be nothing," she mutters. She's not really listening to me. She's focused on the orange glitter.

"Or?" I ask, fishing for information.

She stands up. "An ore of some kind, maybe?"

"An ore?" I breathe. I'd never thought about the mineral resources here. On Earth, even some of the worst places sometimes held unimaginable wealth in the form of rare metals, minerals, or oil. I don't need unimaginable. 'Pretty good' would do. With that, we could buy food and medicine, and maybe even fix the houses.

"You're going back to the Dungeons?" Hailey asks. She continues before I can answer, "I'll come with you."

"Are you ready now?" I ask, excited for her involvement.

We backtrack to where Mirk found me. I'd gotten lucky when I chucked Elias out the crack and stumbled after him. We landed on a ledge about one-third the way up the mountainside.

There's an orange streak on the stones beneath it, trailing down the mountain to run under the rocks. A streak that matches the dust found on my boot.

Hailey and I follow the trail through the boulders, and with every step, the glitter thickens until we reach a section where the ground has cracked into three-foot crevices. At the bottom of each hole, there's heaps of the stuff, mixed with the soil.

I dig with the heel of my boot, pulling out more of the orange dust. "Must be tons under there."

Hailey straightens from where she's jumped into one of the holes and looks at where I'm pointing. "Fascinating."

"Maybe it's worth something? Can you melt it down and test it?" I ask.

"Already on it." She grins as she tosses a sack of dirt at my feet, jumps out of the hole, and pats a pouch of bags hanging off her belt. "I always come prepared."

We collect a few more samples and then head back to Hailey's shop.

She's ready to get to work, and I have preparations to make, but I find myself hesitant to leave. Already I feel at home with her.

She smiles as if she understands and pats me on the shoulder in a slightly awkward way. "I'll have your exploration equipment ready in the morning. And maybe sometime soon we can chat some more over wine and a game of dice."

I grin. "I'd like that."

"YOU'VE ONLY JUST RECOVERED," LADRON objects, his lean jaw jutting at a mutinous angle as he leans against an oak tree. "Mapping the Dungeons is dangerous work."

Mirk analyzes me from under furrowed brows as Torak's wolf eyes narrow. Both of them are reclining on boulders, though Torak looks ready to shift and run wild at any moment.

I level a look at all three of them. "I'm stronger than I've ever been."

And it's the truth. I can feel it all the way to the marrow of my bones. "I know you're only opposing me because you're worried, but I'm fully recovered and ready." To prove the point, I draw my sword and stalk over to Ladron, gently nudging him in the chest. "I'll duel to prove it."

His eyes flicker with a challenging light and he nods. In a blink, his sword is unsheathed and he's on the attack.

It all seems so familiar somehow. Instinct possesses me and I just let it flow. With my right hand, I arc my blade to deflect his blow and with my left, I grab my whip, twist the leather and snake it across the handle of his sword.

The sun catches his blade as it arcs high in the air.

It's only when I'm done that I realize I've just disarmed Hermes—*the Hermes*—in under three seconds.

Mirk chuckles.

Torak grins and begins to clap.

Ladron is staring at me, his brows drawn in surprise. "Where did you learn that?" he asks.

"Instinct." I say, but there's a thread of gravity in his expression that draws me instantly into a more serious mood. "Why?"

He glances at the sword and then his shoulders relax. "Ah, yes. Prometheus' weapons." He smiles.

He puzzles me, but knowing I've won the argument chases all other thoughts away. "Any other challengers?" I tease, cocking a brow at Torak and Mirk.

Mirk's silver eyes glitter as he executes the perfect bow with a flourish. "Shall we head to the Dungeons, my lady?"

A short time later, we stand before one of the many narrow fissures in the cliff wall. While Torak and I were in bed recovering, Mirk and Ladron were exploring the outer levels of the Dungeons to find any leaks and attempt to seal them.

"This one leads directly to an inner level yet to be searched," Ladron says as we step through the crack.

I hold Hailey's lantern aloft. It actually works better than a flashlight. She's used some kind of highly polished reflective metal, and the light burns so brightly it's like I've captured a star in my hand.

The cavern is vast, and on the far side are several tunnels all leading to unfathomable black holes.

"Well, boys, there's no time like the present." With nervous excitement pulsing through, I take a step into the unknown.

WE SPEND THE DAY EXPLORING. THE DUNGEONS are huge, far bigger than I ever imagined. And strangely empty, except the piles of animal bones near the entrances, leftovers from the manticore's feasting. From time to time, I think I hear the scraping of many legs, but when I shine the lamp in the direction of the sound, there's nothing there.

"Just how deep is this place?" I ask, glancing down at the map I'm drawing as we go. We've headed down another level, and still there's no end in sight. "Surely, Prometheus can't be too far off. Ladron, you helped capture the monsters, right?"

"Yes, but I've never been inside," he says, running his hand along the passage wall. "Prometheus brought the cages here himself."

We venture further, but it's just more of the same, our lanterns shining brightly against the now familiar backdrop of dark, narrow passageways, low ceilings, cobwebs, and bones.

We end the day with no monsters sighted and no sign of Prometheus.

The next day is more of the same.

And the next.

A week passes, and I'm heading out for another exciting day of Dungeon mapping when Hailey catches us on our way out of town from the palace.

I can tell by the excited gleam in her eyes that she has good news.

"What is it?" I ask, already smiling in anticipation.

"It's incredible." She's grinning so widely I can see all of her teeth. "So unique. You've got to see this." She pulls out a small garden trowel from the leather satchel on her shoulder and nods at the dry, rocky soil at our feet. "Try it out."

I squint at the small tool. It's unusually light, easy to handle. Sending Hailey a curiously amused look, I crouch and drag the trowel over the dirt.

It cuts through the soil—and rocks—like butter.

I blink.

Torak gives a low whistle.

"Astounding," Ladron says. "A sword of that metal could, perhaps, cut through even Poseidon's Trident."

Hailey chuckles. "That's the beauty of all this," she says.

"No." I frown, standing my ground. "I said no weapons."

Hailey's still smiling. "Hold out your hands, Lily."

I'm still frowning, but I cup my palms.

She takes a small bag from her satchel, unties the leather strings, and dumps the glittery ore into my hands. "This is yours. Your land. And because of it, the soil reflects your intention. You don't want this ore to be used to build weapons, so it won't allow itself to be. I tried, believe me. I spent the last week attempting to create every manner of weaponry imaginable. But I couldn't." She pauses, letting that sink in before she adds, "This ore only forms into gardening tools, harnesses, lamps, nails—items of use. Anything but weapons."

I stare in wonder at the small garden trowel.

"It's a one of a kind metal. Unmatched. And yes,

Ladron, it's stronger than even Poseidon's trident," she says.

I shiver as a new thought comes to mind. "It's a darn good thing Zeus didn't give these lands to someone who's keen on waging war," I say. Like Clay. Imagine what he'd do with such ore. I don't want to think about that, so I force my thoughts onto the positive, the promising. "Maybe we can sell a few tools and lamps to get money for improvements." Healers. Food. Cy and the other children are so scrawny. Fresh fruit and vegetables would do them good.

"I'll get on that right away," Hailey says, snagging the trowel from my hand and stuffing it into her satchel. "I've already started sketching several new designs. I think you'll be pleased."

I reach out and pull her into a hug. "I already am. You're an incredible blacksmith," I say.

She doesn't respond, but she swipes at her eyes and sniffs inconspicuously, before turning away.

A genuine smile lights up my face, and for the first time, I feel a real sense of hope. I wave to my men. "Ready? We've got Dungeons to map."

Two days later, Hailey makes the first sale and returns home over the mountains with a bag full of gold. We hire men from our village to dig and deliver the ore to her shop, where banging can be heard at all hours of the day and night.

I don't think she sleeps, so engrossed with her work as she is.

When she leaves again, she carries a much larger stock of custom items useful for all manner of duties.

With the second bag of gold comes the first wagon of supplies.

The days march on and turn into weeks. A trade route is established. Each week, a wagon of tools and lamps leave to return filled with bricks, grain, fruit, and medicine.

And each evening I walk through the village with Ladron, Torak and Mirk, on our way back from another day of mapping the Dungeons, I start to notice a roof repaired, or a group of children running through the street playing instead of coughing in the corners.

Then, one day, it happens. I stand next to my palace looking out over my queendom and I feel it, the deep-rooted sense of belonging to this place. It's a deeper level than what the mere word of 'home' can convey.

It's my land. My people. We're in this together. We all belong.

Tears mist my eyes.

"And what plays so heavily on your mind?" Mirk asks, slowly fading into view before me.

"These are good tears," I say, looking up at him.

Over the past few weeks, I've gotten closer to all of them. Torak, of course, slips into my bed more often than not, but my attraction for him hasn't lessened my growing feelings for the other men.

Mirk says nothing as he lifts his thumb to wipe the tear from my cheek. I step closer to him and place my palm on his chest.

Slowly, I tilt my face up to his, expecting him to whisper as he always does, 'You're not ready for me, yet.'

But this time, there's a look in those silver eyes that arrests all other thoughts. A look of wanting. Desire. Mirk, unmasked.

I hold still lest the spell should break.

A slight breeze whirls around us, teasing his dark hair as slowly, his mouth dips towards mine.

Though his lips still hover a few inches from mine, already, my knees grow weak.

I close my eyes.

"Tidings," Ladron's voice cuts through the lust-filled air.

I jerk and turn as Mirk steps back.

It's Ladron, striding towards us, the tic on his lean jaw warning me his tidings aren't the good kind.

"What is it?" I ask.

"There," he says, pointing to the opposite side of the mountain.

We follow him to a new vantagepoint that offers a different view of the road.

There's a party approaching, winding their way up the hill to the palace.

I freeze.

It's Zeus.

And at his right hand, riding a white Arabian stallion, and wearing a gold-trimmed black tunic, is Clay.

18

"Do NOT SPOIL what you have by desiring what you have not; remember that what you now have was once among the things you only hoped for." ~Epicurus

A DOZEN NYMPHS RUN BEFORE THE GODS TO litter rose petals on the ground leading to my palace entrance. Muscled warriors wearing the emblem of Clay's house arrive to plant their black banners in the ground as they line the rose-strewn path. I only have time to wonder why Clay brought so many servants before both he and Zeus dismount from their gold bedecked Arabians.

I stride forward to greet them with Ladron and Mirk by my side as more gods and goddesses begin to arrive, some on horses, some on litters beaded with bronze, silver, and gold and born by servants wearing soft robes. Hades. Poseidon. Athena. Narcissus. Morpheus. Arcas.

There's more, but I quit looking as Zeus in his golden robes and Clay in his black come to a stop before me.

"Zeus," I greet him with a nod of my head and pointedly ignore Clay.

Zeus towers over me, but he's not making eye contact. He looks straight past Ladron as if he doesn't exist and locks his gaze on a particularly winsome nymph who's fluttering come-hither lashes. "Refreshment," he booms, distracted. "And make my quarters ready." He shrugs and moves as if to stride right past me, treating me like an insignificant gnat.

"We don't have feasts here," I say, anger ripping the words straight out of my soul. I'm not his servant. I'm a goddess. A queen. And he's in my queendom now. I'm not taking much-needed food from my people's mouths.

Zeus stops midstride and turns back to me, and for the first time, I feel the full force of his attention. He's overwhelming, his gray eyes electric storms of power.

I want to step back, but I force myself to hold my

ground. "My people can scarcely afford to feed them-selves," I explain. Looking over just how many he brought in this party, a single Olympus-caliber feast would provide food for my queendom for months. "We've no need for sustenance, I'll not starve them for the entertainment of the gods."

Zeus' face flushes a dark red, but before he unleashes his anger, Athena steps in front of her father and agrees, "That is wise, Lily. Your land will only flourish through the labor of your people, and for that, they must eat." She waves at the line of servants still trailing up the road toward the palace. "I'm happy to donate a portion of my provisions to allow the good people here to celebrate." She leans over to where Narcissus, Morpheus, and several other gods are standing behind her on the rose-strewn path. "As I'm sure, you will, as well?"

Narcissus looks put out, but he clearly doesn't want to be outdone by Athena, so he agrees. Morpheus and the others begrudgingly follow suit.

As Zeus storms past me, I surrender my objec-tions. "Then, a feast there shall be," I say as the party flows into the palace.

Hades seems to be in a bad mood. He draws his crimson cloak around his shoulders and strides past, pointedly ignoring Mirk—his son—standing at my side. A quick glance at Mirk's face tells me he's used to such treatment. It's clear why he values the importance of family. He's never had one himself, if how his father treats him is any indication. No wonder it would seem the most precious of gifts to him, and he's not wrong. My heart squeezes at the thought of my own family back on Earth. My mind drifts there less often of late, but the weight of their loss still holds heavy in my soul.

Poseidon arrives next. His purple tunic hangs off one shoulder to reveal an impressive set of abs—like father, like son—and his pauldrons and leggings are studded with sapphires and amethyst. He strolls toward my palace with each arm tucked around the waist of a rose-petal-dropping nymph. When he catches sight of his son, he stops in surprise.

Torak shifts almost imperceptibly.

"Torak?" Poseidon laughs, his sea-blue eyes twinkling. He raises his voice and shouts after Zeus. "You didn't mention my half-breed pup was here."

Torak lifts a cool brow. "Father," he greets in a neutral tone.

Poseidon chuckles and then sweeps the nymphs forward. "This goddess is even lower than I thought if Zeus tossed her that old bone."

I flush with anger on Torak's behalf, but he

doesn't seem upset. He drops a strong hand on my shoulder and gives me a comforting squeeze.

Or maybe it's a squeeze meant to stay my sudden rage.

It works, more or less.

Still irritated, I prepare to follow the gods inside when I see Aphrodite heading down the rose-petal walkway. She's wearing a simple white tunic and a circlet of golden leaves in her hair, but she's so beautiful, she needs nothing else. She detours to where Clay is standing about twenty feet away, surveying the palace. As she slips up behind him to slide her arm through his, he leans to whisper something in her ear. She giggles, and it's that laugh that gives it away. They're together. Like, together together.

Really? I thought Aphrodite was smarter than that. Couldn't she see straight through Clay's despicable, transparent soul? And what about Hailey's father —her husband—Hephaestus? I guess she dropped the old blacksmith after her reincarnation.

Scowling, I wheel around and march into my palace.

Athena steals Ladron the instant we step through the door. "Let's catch up, Brother. You don't mind, do you, Lily?" she asks with a bright smile. "Hermes and I haven't spoken in some time."

"Please, visit," I say. "And thank you," I add, before she walks off with Ladron. "For siding with me."

A mischievous grin pulls at her lips. "It may look like an old boy's club here, but we goddesses wield more power than they realize. Be assured of that."

Ladron and Athena walk away arm in arm, talking with their heads bent close together. Ladron glances back at me and winks before disappearing into the hordes of servants carrying platters of edibles, bolts of cloth, baskets of fresh flowers, and spools of gold wire and ribbon. It's crazy. I step out of the way as a line of men carrying huge wooden crates struggle past.

One of them tips and Torak steps forward to give them a helping hand.

"What's in there? Elephants?" I ask waspishly as they disappear toward the feasting room.

I hear a snort behind me. It's Hades, leaning against the wall, his arms folded across his chest. When I glance back at my side, it's to see Mirk has already disappeared.

"I know what it's like," Hades tells me with a sarcastic smile.

"What?" I ask, torn about actually stepping closer to talk to him. He's Hades, after all. Hades.

"Getting a shit kingdom," he says with a bit of an eye roll.

"I suppose you of all gods would be most familiar with that. What did you do to turn yours around?" I ask.

He barks out an unhappy laugh. "Turn it around? There's no turning this around, little girl. You got shit on by Zeus and you'll have to wallow in it. Happens to the best of us."

He walks away without another word and I shake my head. Of all the Greek gods I read about on Earth, I never expected to relate to Hades the most—taking Hermes out of the equation, anyway.

I head up to my room to find a soft blue silk gown on the bed, trimmed with coral beads. The gladiator sandals are twisted with fine gold. It's elegant, delicate. Ladron's handiwork, no doubt. The silk slips over my shoulders, caressing my skin. The last thing in the world I want to do is feast with arrogant gods, but I need to find out what Zeus and Clay are doing here. Nothing good, I know that for a fact. How bad is the real question.

When I return, my palace has been transformed into a mini version of Zeus' opulent feasts on Mount Olympus.

Mirk is waiting for me at the bottom of the staircase, his dark eyes lidded, watchful, and his loose blue tunic falling open to showcase his abs beneath. There's more than one nymph eyeing him, and I can't blame them. He's definitely fun to look at.

When I descend to the bottom step, Mirk caresses my body with a slow, lazy gaze so warm it's like he's touching my skin.

With a flirtatious glint in his eyes, he steps up to offer me an arm, and we make our way to the feasting hall, walking under the chains of flowers strung across the colonnades. Vines trail down the stone columns and here and there, potted fig trees cluster around various statues, all Zeus, each marble monument a testament to some victory in battle. Since this is my house, I know these statues weren't there this morning, which mean Zeus travels with his own supply. It speaks volumes about his ego. I mean, who does that?

I don't even recognize my own feasting hall.

They've filled the pool running down the center. Water nymphs sit at the edge now, braiding wreaths of flowers as they laugh and sing.

The walls are draped in purple and gold banners trimmed with amethyst beads. Zeus' guards stand in their gold armor as musicians play their lyres and flutes. Around them tree nymphs dance, contorting their flexible bodies into impossible shapes.

I see Aphrodite, her hair is now twisted up with golden pins studded in rubies, with lapis and diamonds dripping from her necklace, and several bracelets jangling on her wrists. Her gown is a shimmer of gold sparkles, glistening in the torchlight and her strappy mid-calf gladiator sandals are braided with gold.

She's talking to Thetis, the mother of Achilles, and an ancient goddess of the sea who looks more my age. She's a lot taller, though, and a bit of a punk in the fashion department. Granted, her hair is naturally green, but instead of the typical goddess style of long, curly waves, she's shaved her head close to her scalp. Her ears are studded with rings and her left nostril is even pierced with a gold stud, topped with coral. She's dressed in black leather that accentuates her curves to perfection as she moves with the lithesome grace of a dancer.

The fragrance of rose oil wafts through the torch-lit air as Mirk and I weave our way through the crowd, catching snippets of gossip.

"Did you hear about Erysichthon's son? Cut another sacred grove down to build onto his palace. He can't even afford what he has, just like his father..."

Two nymphs giggle as one says, "Now that

Aphrodite is back, think she'll regain her place as reigning beauty or will..."

We move on, the music of lyres and flutes a constant backdrop, filtering through the buzz of the gods' voices as they carry on their conversations.

"Did Zeus really invite his son to this feast?"

"Hermes?"

"No, the son he had with that nymph."

"The one with the red hair?"

"No, the one where he turned himself into the goose..."

"I thought Hera killed that one with snakes?"

"No, that was..."

They could probably go on all night with that conversation. Looks like even the gods are losing track of Zeus' sons.

When we reach the couches arranged at the head of the pool, Mirk leans down, his lips brushing my ear as he murmurs, "Alas, I must leave you here."

I look up to object, but he's already gone, and then I see why. Hades is lurking nearby. But he's not looking at me, his eyes are tracking something in the air and after a moment, he pushes himself off the wall as if he's following. Looks like Hades can see through Mirk's invisibility. Just who is avoiding who, I wonder?

I sit on my couch and recline against my pillows to wait for Zeus. A wood nymph hands me a goblet of golden nectar, and I taste the shimmering liquid with the tip of my tongue. It's mind-blowing, a mix of floral, honey, and liquid gold, and deep inside, the goddess in me stirs, sighing in pleasure to once again drink something so long denied.

Denied? The thought startles me, and I know it's a memory of the past—the life I had here, before I died and was reborn human.

Soon, one day, I might remember my past god life. Who I am.

But do I want to?

Looking down at the long line of gods and goddesses lounging on their couches, lips stained gold with nectar, I wonder what kind of goddess I had been. One who treated humans as insects? The decadent indulgence surrounding me stands in stark contrast to the conditions of my kingdom. If I could get even a fraction of what is here, I could improve the lives of my people permanently.

"So nice to see you again, Lady Lily."

I mentally groan. Clay. Would I ever get away from him?

He's standing behind me in a tunic with a golden

disc around his neck so extravagant he outshines nearly every god in attendance.

"Can't even say hi to an old friend?" Clay asks, searching my face.

But the reflexive 'no' in my eyes is clear. I make sure of it.

He sighs heavily and adopts an apologetic demeanor—straight down to fake puppy dog eyes. "Fair enough, Lily. I deserve that. I was an ass on Earth."

"Just on Earth?" I snort. "What about the cyclops?"

"Hey, I thought you were embarrassed," he says. "You know, old friends just helping each other out. Let me make it up to you. Come now, Lil, can't we be friends? We're going to be here a long time. Very long. We're gods after all."

I'm spared from answering by Zeus' entrance.

It's quite the fanfare as he makes his way through the room to the purple-swathed golden couch at the head of the pool, two couches from mine.

As he arrives, I step forward to greet him, but he cuts me down with a look and strides straight past me.

This isn't good.

A nymph kneels before him with a pearl-studded

golden cup of nectar. He takes a hearty draught and then lifts his hand.

The feasting room falls silent.

"Welcome," he says, still holding his cup aloft. "As more monsters are released into the world, I've decided new leadership is needed to protect all lands. Tonight, I asked you here to celebrate Epimetheus, a god who has proven a hero who can handle these challenges and responsibilities…"

It's only then that his words sink in.

Clay? Zeus was really here, giving Clay my queendom?

"This is an outrage—" I hear Ladron roaring.

I see him, but my mind is awhirl. Clay won't take care of my people. They'll go back to starving. He won't give them medical care. And the Dungeons? He doesn't have the guts to live right by the front door. He's a coward. The only thing he excels at is running. So, why? And why now?

"Tomorrow, Clay will be crowned," Zeus raises his voice to thunder above the buzz in the feasting hall.

Why is this happening? I glance at Clay's smug smile and glance down at his hands. At the goblet he holds.

A goblet Hailey made recently and sold.

A goblet forged from the magical ore found in my dirt.

This is worse than I imagined. With Clay as ruler, his intention will be far different from mine. It's about more than my people, my land. It's about everyone.

"The Dungeons are too dangerous for the likes of Clay," Ladron is saying.

"This is my decision." Zeus pounds his fist on the table beside his couch. The rose-quartz bowl of ambrosia resting there shatters into pieces.

"Is it?" Ladron challenges. "This queendom was given to Lily. Her name was written on your scroll."

"True, that," Hades chimes in from where he's lounging against the wall.

Zeus cuts him a dark look.

I know this is my chance. Zeus is going to find a way to give Clay these lands, anyway, so I really don't have anything to lose.

I think fast, piecing together everything I know about Zeus.

What can I do to turn the tide in my favor? Or at least give me a chance at keeping my queendom.

What do gods care about even more than power?

Their pride.

I have my answer.

I raise my voice as I stand before Zeus. "I propose a duel," I say, my voice confident. "If Clay is truly the strongest and bravest choice to defend this land, he'll have no trouble besting me in a duel. Yes?"

Athena claps. "What a wonderful idea."

Poseidon gives a bored yawn. "A duel is a damn sight more entertaining than this mess," he grumbles.

"A duel," Hades says with a nod. "Brilliant."

Zeus turns his glare on me, obviously irritated at my challenge, but as the rest of the gods begin to wager over who will win, he knows better than to disagree at this point. "So, it's settled. Tomorrow at dawn, you will duel."

Relieved, I return to my couch.

Clay gives me the Evil Eye before a confident mask slips over his face. Keeping his gaze on me, he leans over to assure Aphrodite, "This will be easy. Tomorrow, I'll squeeze Lily dry like the old, shriveled lemon she is."

I let his words fertilize the vengeance growing in my heart. Clay may not know it yet, but tomorrow I will make lemonade out of his head.

[19]

"From the deepest desires often come the deadliest hate." ~Socrates

"Clay fights dirty," Mirk says as he blinks into existence at my side. "I've been watching him practice."

The guys and I found a private spot in the woods outside the palace grounds to prepare for the duel away from prying eyes.

"I'd expect nothing else from him," I say, lowering my sword. I don't point out the slight hypocrisy in his accusation, given he was just spying on Clay.

"As far as skills go, he cuts his strokes short," Mirk continues. "He doesn't follow through."

"Sounds like Clay," I grunt, feinting right and then leaping left against an imaginary partner. "He excels at doing half-assed jobs. Still, I'm not going to count on that. I'm not taking chances. Not with so much riding on this fight."

Torak growls.

Ladron clenches his jaw even tighter.

All three men are unhappy, and despite the stress of the situation, their bristling protectiveness makes me smile. The sky is still dark in the east, but soon, Helios will bring the sun and the duel will start, deciding my queendom's fate.

"You're allowed only one weapon, so let's make it count," Ladron says. He unsheathes his sword and steps up to me, looking like he has so much more to say and to teach, like he intends to cram centuries of experience into the little time we have left. "Remember, the first one to knock the other out of the circle wins. So, use your wit and the boundaries to your advantage. Let's practice."

For the next hour, we thrust, cut, feint and parry, all the while dancing around a crudely drawn circle in an attempt to force each other to step outside the line.

Finally, as the morning mist settles around us, I drop my sword. "Enough."

Ladron nods and steps back, wiping the sweat from his brow. "Thank you," he says, a smile quirking the corner of his lip.

"What for?"

He nods his chin at my sword. "This fight. You're exceptionally skilled. I feel like I'm fighting an old friend, one I've missed sorely."

"It's time," Mirk announces, his gaze trained on the heavens above.

The first ray of light is breaking the horizon to streak the sky pink.

"I'm ready," I say, and I hope to all the gods, Greek or otherwise, that it's true.

Alfio joins us as we leave our makeshift training area for the site of the duel. He struggles to match our pace as he says, "Do not let fear become your enemy, m'lady. Focus on Clay, not fear. Fear only feeds itself in a fight like this. You are in control, m'queen. Let fear run only as deep as you allow. Just concentrate on your opponent, and forget to be afraid."

I look at him, surprised. "Forget to be afraid," I say. "I like that."

He smiles at me and slows his pace, his bones too old to keep up. I shake my head and keep walking, marveling on the enigma that is Alfio. When this is over, I want to sit down and have a deeper chat with him. Maybe over an ale.

The sky is bathed in pink and gold as we arrive at a newly formed amphitheater built for the gods overnight. No wonder they travel with an army of servants and wagons of shit.

There's another rose-petal walkway with three more marble statues of Zeus, one on either side of the amphitheater entrance, and another placed beside a raised dais holding a single golden couch. For Zeus, obviously. There are half a dozen nymphs ready and waiting for him, holding bowls of ambrosia, fruit, and goblets of nectar.

Around the arena, other couches are arranged on carpets, each with their respective cluster of servants ready to attend their deity.

Hailey sits in the corner. When she sees me, she stands on her feet and shouts, "Go, Team Lily."

Her energy is contagious and activates that ancient part of me, the goddess residing deep within. The one I'm beginning to recognize. The one who knew how to throw that spear and the same one who's comfortable wielding a sword.

I walk into the arena, noting that the circle in the center is made of gold dust. After this is over, I'll have the dust sifted to remove all the gold. There's enough here to fix a few houses. Maybe even buy an ox to plow the fields I'm going to make.

On either side of the circle is a mark where Clay and I are obviously supposed to stand. I move to the one closest to Hailey and glance around.

Hades is directly opposite of me. He gives me a curt nod as our eyes connect and then, there's a rising murmur in the gathering crowd and I look over to see Zeus has arrived on his dais.

He sits and a holds out a hand. As a nymph hurries to give him a golden cup of nectar, he looks out over the amphitheater. I can tell by the way his jaw juts that he's still pissed. I've definitely landed on his shit list.

A cheer breaks out, drawing my eyes back to the entrance, and Clay stalks into the arena, resplendent in black leather embroidered with gold.

My stomach clenches.

This is it. Shit is about to get real.

It's Clay, after all. He's gotten me killed before. In fact, he's won every encounter with me so far, though not by the rules, of course. He's cheated each time and still walked away the victor. One wrong move, and I'll lose everything, and not just me, but also the people who live here, the ones who depend on me.

I draw a shaky breath, but then I hear Alfio's words whisper through my mind: Forget to be afraid.

Right.

Still, I grip my sword handle, tight, as Clay heads my way.

His expression is one of cold calculation and it's striking, reminding me I'm better served to treat him as the god he is now, not the conniving student he was on Earth. If I remember skills from my previous godhood, then clearly, he does, too.

"Forget to be afraid," I whisper under my breath as he takes his place.

Zeus stands up. "Let the duel begin," he says without preamble.

A horn sounds.

We circle each other, cautiously eyeing the other for weaknesses.

"It's not too late to back out, Lil," says Clay, his voice smooth and calm. "I don't want to hurt you—" He strikes out, trying to catch me off guard.

But I step out of the way, the heat of his blade on my skin as my hair blows back from my face.

It's then the strength in me ignites, like a flicker of flame that's doused with gasoline. I explode in power, twisting and attacking. Clay is slow to block, and my blade slices his sleeve, nicking his flesh.

He swears and steps back, golden ichor welling from the cut.

"First blood," the gods call out, clearly enjoying their entertainment.

"Go, Lily, go!" Hailey shouts.

"That was a mistake," Clay hisses at me. "So, you want to play dirty?"

His nostrils flare in anger, and he attacks again.

Our swords clang, rasp, and spark as he channels his rage into a series of deadly assaults, each one meant to maim, each one forcing me to fall back under the weight of his attack. Then, he swings too wide, and as he arcs his sword to deliver another blow, I manage to deflect his strike and twist away.

He grins, his eyes dropping to the dirt.

Shit. I forgot about the circle. I'm perilously close to the edge. It's hard to keep track of it all.

The horn sounds again and we separate, each returning to our respective mark.

The gods are enjoying themselves, laughing and sipping wine and nectar as they lay bets on the winner. Apparently, I've surprised them. They're much more animated now.

"He favors his right," Ladron says as he arrives with a goblet of nectar. "He's sloppy. When he attacks, he leaves his torso wide open."

"Doesn't feel too sloppy," I mumble before downing my nectar.

Strength courses through me. As I hand Ladron the empty goblet and wipe my mouth with the back of my hand, I notice my people in the amphitheater, crowding close amongst the servants. As our eyes meet, they raise their hands in salute and dip their heads in respect. They know I'm fighting for them. They know what's at stake as much as I do. Even Cy is here, waving at me, a cheeky grin on his face, and my heart swells at the support. I can't let him down. I can't let any of them down.

The horn sounds again in warning that our break is over.

"You can do this," Ladron says, cupping my cheek. "I don't doubt that for a second."

For an infinite moment, I stand there, acutely aware of his caress, his nearness, drawing strength from his conviction, and then, time returns with a rush. He leaves and I turn to face Clay.

Aphrodite has delivered his nectar and she's giving him a final kiss, her hands sliding over his chest and around his belt. The sun has risen high enough that the beams catch on the many rings covering her hands. The flash of metal makes me glance away, and then she's running across the arena to her couch to watch.

The horn sounds once more.

This is it.

Clay doesn't wait. He's on a mission, bearing down on me with the force of a maddened bull, and this time, I really do forget to be afraid. Alfio was right. It just gets in the way.

When he attacks, I'm ready. Ladron's observations were spot on. He does leave himself unprotected. My blade slashes across his midriff.

He grunts in shock, then swears as anger contorts his face. Fueled by rage, his blade arcs in even wilder swings as I dodge and dance out of the way, taking advantage of his mental state to entice him towards the circle's edge. Then, it'll be game over.

When he lunges, I'm ready. With a flick of my wrist, he's disarmed, his sword flashing in the sun.

He swears and dives for me headlong, tackling me to the ground, using his weight to pin me down. I jam the hilt of my sword into his ribs, and we roll to the side, me on top now, my blade aimed at his throat. "Yield," I yell.

He reaches for something in his cloak, and then I feel the heat pierce my flesh. My stomach spasms.

A dagger.

Clay brought two weapons. He's cheating. Again.

I drag a shuddering breath as pain fires through flesh, muscle and deeper. I can feel the blood spreading across my abdomen, warm and sticky.

"You'll never beat me," says Clay. He puts his foot against my chest, and with one powerful kick, launches me into the air.

And over the line.

Mid-air, time moves slowly, and as the ground nears, I can see Hailey, shocked, mouth wide open. Ladron, Mirk and Torak, heads hanging low. And I think of all the people I am about to fail. Cy, Cora. Alfio. I was never their hero. I was never anything special. They should have left me behind. Like my father did. They should have left me.

They...

A swirl of memories rush over me.

Memories of saving Elias from the manticore.

Memories of chatting with Ladron, Mirk and Torak around a campfire.

Memories of laughing with my mom, dad and sisters.

And I realize, none of those moments would have been the same without me. None of those moments would have been special.

Make lemonade of his head, Lily.

I lunge my sword into the ground, burying the blade's tip into the earth. Still in the air, I use my strength to slow myself down. To stay balanced on the hilt of my weapon. My body never touches the dirt. And with all my strength I push backwards, launching away from my sword.

And back into the circle.

Clay looks at me, eyes wide, face pale. And before he can react, I kick him in the side, and he flips over the line, rolling in the dust.

THE CROWD ERUPTS WITH CHEERING AND clapping. People begin chanting my name. *Lily. Lily. Lily!*

I raise my sword in triumph, grinning madly.

It takes a moment for the reality to set in. I won. I saved my people, despite Clay cheating. I've secured my queendom for good.

Then the pain in my abdomen flares as the adrenaline leaves my body, and I double over, clutching my stomach with shaking hands.

Ladron is the first to reach me. His jaw clenches tight as he places his palms over my wound to staunch the flow of blood. I glance down at the gold seeping between his fingers.

Torak is at my side next. "Here, let me see," He drops to his knees beside me and takes a small silver bag from his belt, and as he pulls it open, he gives me a comforting smile. "Herbs from the forest. They'll set you to rights by nightfall." His smile turns briefly to an apologetic frown. "It'll sting, though."

It does.

I bite down on my lip as my body burns.

Mirk appears at my side, holding my hand. "We're here for you, Lily. Always."

Zeus speaks through the roar of the crowd. "Silence now. I will have silence."

But the people do not relent. Instead they only cheer louder.

Zeus continues all the same. "The girl cheated. You saw her body outside the ring. I pronounce Epimetheus, winner of the duel and King of the Dungeons!"

I raise my head to face him, my face drained of blood and not just because I'm literally leaking the stuff. "There's only one cheater here," I yell. With the last of my strength, I stand and walk over to Clay, Ladron, Torak, and Mirk helping me move.

"What do you want?" hisses Clay.

I reach out with my hand, into his cloak, too quick for him to stop me, and draw out the dagger. I hold it high for all to see. The blade is still covered in my blood.

For three seconds, no one speaks.

"The bastard," Hailey yells.

"A shameful disgrace," Poseidon lifts his voice, driving his trident into the ground to emphasize his words.

As the ground rumbles in response, Athena rises from her couch next to Zeus. "Disgusting," she says to Clay. "You have shown no honor."

The gods murmur agreement. All except Zeus.

And Clay begins to tremble. "It's a trick. She planted the dagger on me. She—"

"Be silent," roars Zeus. "You fool. You have made a mockery of yourself. I should have never supported you." Already, the great god distances himself from this disgrace.

Athena raises her hands, speaking to the crowd. "By breaking the rules of this duel, Epimetheus has forfeited all rights to this kingdom. The Land of the Dungeons belongs to Queen Lily, and Queen Lily alone."

Clay's face flushes red with anger, and he storms away, pushing through the crowd.

Ladron slides a strong, supporting arm under my shoulders and helps me to walk over to a couch. Torak's herbs are powerful, indeed. I can already feel my flesh knitting back together again.

"Easy," Mirk cautions, holding his hands out as if Ladron might drop me at any moment.

Ladron scowls at him. "I will not let her fall."

"I'm fine, you guys," I say. "Just a little sore."

As we head for the palace, cheers of "Queen Lily" begin to echo, mixing with various snippets of conversation from the gods.

"A right entertaining duel. Haven't had so much fun in ages."

"Capital entertainment, but I saw the dagger coming…"

Entertainment? That's all this was to them? No wonder Ladron believes mortals and gods don't mix.

I turn my focus away from the gods and towards my people. They are smiling, happy and confident that I will always fight for them.

As they toss flowers to me, I walk with my back straight into the palace for some rest.

I stretch out in the silk sheets, reveling in

the softness against my skin and the solid warmth against my back. I turn to find Ladron lying next to me. He raises himself on an elbow, and peers down at me, his gaze filled with such heat that I slide my arms around his neck and pull him towards my lips.

His response is gentle, slow, and spine-tinglingly deep, a kiss of carefully harnessed control. I moan, wanting all of him unleashed, but at the sound, he pulls away. "You must heal first, *Lilyitsa*," he whispers.

I'm disappointed, but I know he's right. A few hours rest has done wonders, but my injury is still there.

"How long have I slept?" I ask. I fell asleep nearly the instant he helped me to my bed.

"Just a few hours." His blue eyes are filled with so many emotions. Relief. Desire. Pride. And there's a hesitancy there, too, one that puzzles me.

"What is it?" I ask, tracing the crease in his jaw with a fingertip.

He draws a long breath. "There's something… something I need to tell you," he begins.

A sharp knock on the door interrupts us and before I can respond, Athena sweeps inside with an armful of blue and silver silk. "You're awake! How wonderful," she grins. "Out, Ladron. Lily is late for the feast. Zeus is almost ready to head down."

"Feast?" I ask, sitting up slowly.

"A celebration of your victory," she explains, laying a splendid gown on the foot of the bed to smooth out a skirt sparkling with seed pearls. "It's ready. They're waiting."

I look at Ladron. He'd been about to tell me something important.

"It'll wait," he whispers, swinging his feet off the bed.

As he vanishes through the door, I turn to Athena. "Another feast?"

"Compliments of Clay." She gives a silvery tinkle of a laugh. "He lost. It's only fitting that he pays the bill, don't you think?"

I grin and get ready.

It doesn't take long before I'm following Athena down the stairs. At the bottom, Torak, Ladron, and Mirk wait for me, each sexy and handsome in their own way.

As Athena leads me past, they fall into step behind us as escorts.

The palace decorations have changed from the night before. Now there's an abundance of lilies that I'm sure are in my honor. And yet even more marble statues of Zeus, ones I haven't seen before, and I've seen a dozen unique ones by now. Who travels with their own supply of marble selfies?

There are two golden couches at the head of the pool this time, the larger one obviously belonging to Zeus. As Athena takes me to the smaller one on the right, my heart sinks.

"You're not making me sit next to him, are you?" I grumble at her as we arrive.

"Don't worry. Hermes and the others will stand behind you, and I'll be there," Athena laughs, pointing to the couch on my left. "He's grumpy. He doesn't like to lose, so I wouldn't dream of leaving you alone with him."

I give her a look, but I'm suddenly tired, so I quit objecting and sit down.

As the men arrange themselves behind me, Zeus arrives.

I stand along with the rest as Zeus takes his place. He doesn't give a speech to announce my queendom, but he does grace me with a curt nod.

Once the feast begins, Zeus proceeds to ignore me, but I don't mind. In fact, I'm relieved. I'm just tired of dealing with him. He's caught so deep in the web of superiority that he'll never listen to me. And from the looks Hades is sending his way, I can see it's nothing new.

Athena chatters at my side, teasing me with various stories of the gods I'd never heard before. Like the time Zeus got intimate with a platypus, that baby was a weird creature, Athena tells me with a shocked expression on her face. Or the time Dionysus gave up on wine and instead subsisted on something he called 'White Claw' until several gods intervened, insisting that he go back to normal alcohol after a few really unfortunate incidences that she refuses to share.

The feast marches on, nectar and wine flowing. I'm not really thirsty and I don't have much of an appetite, so I just listen and watch.

When Zeus coughs for the third time I glance over at him curiously. His face seems a little dark and he's frowning. But then, he's been in a bad mood all night.

"Strange," Athena says at my side.

I turn back to continue our conversation, but freeze. Her face is dark as well, an odd shade of purple.

"What is it?" I ask, sitting up.

Ladron joins me at once as Athena begins to cough like Zeus.

I glance down at the end of the long table where Clay is sitting in a place of dishonor, as far from Zeus as possible. I expect to see him sulking, but instead he's whispering to Aphrodite, then they both laugh as if everything went the way they planned.

My stomach clenches, and the hair on my neck stands on end. Something is off.

I scan the room, though I'm not sure what I'm looking for specifically. Then it clicks. All the guards are familiar. I've seen them before. They're Clay's men. They were part of the procession he left Mount Olympus with.

I turn to Athena, my face pinched with worry. "Something is wrong," I tell her.

But Athena doesn't respond. Her face is a bloated purple now and as she coughs, gold ichor foaming at her mouth until she collapses, seizing against the table.

This attracts Zeus' attention. "Daughter," he says, leaning towards Athena. "My daughter."

His words dissolve into fits of coughing as he falls to the side as well.

Poseidon and Hades are the next victims.

Fear grips my heart as god after god succumbs to the same ailment.

Guests begin to scream. "Poison!" someone cries out. "They've been poisoned. Don't drink the wine!"

I study my cup. I drank the wine, but I'm fine.

Why aren't I feeling sick like the others? Clay and Aphrodite had been drinking as well, to no ill effect.

I search for Clay, but he's no longer in his seat.

Instead, he's stalking towards me, pointing his finger in accusation. "It was her, the Dungeon Queen," he roars, filling his voice with righteous indignation. "Her and her men. Hermes stole the arrows of plague and pestilence for her. I heard him boast of it to his friends when he thought I wasn't near. Torak, Mirk, and Hermes. They have poisoned their fathers with the venom from the arrows. And she helped them."

"You lie," I shout, jumping up from my seat. "We need a healer."

"Arrest her!" he yells to his men.

I look around, but all the gods that might have been inclined to help me have succumbed to the poison. It takes a moment for the truth to penetrate my shock, but when I realize what's happening, my blood runs cold. This is a coup. It doesn't matter what I say or do, Clay is overthrowing Mount Olympus, and setting me up to take the blame. The only gods left untouched are on his side already. That's why I didn't get sick.

I'm the scapegoat.

"Run," yells Ladron from his place across the great hall. "*Run!*"

I STUMBLE THROUGH THE DOOR AND INTO THE long hallways of my palace. I clutch my wound, which is once again oozing ichor, leaving a trail behind me. Clay's guards are on my heel, but a white wolf leaps in their way. Torak... he bares his teeth and prepares to fight. He's sacrificing himself so I can escape.

I want to stop and help him, but this has all gone to shit.

Mirk appears from the shadows, disarming two of the guards.

"Go Lily. Go."

"I won't leave you," I shout, brandishing my sword. The movement sends a jolt of pain through my body, and I suck in a breath.

"You must. Go. Find Prometheus. He is the only one who can fix this now," Mirk says.

Tears fill my eyes, and I know he's right, but abandoning them feels like a betrayal. Still, I turn and run, making it outside.

My heart is pounding in my chest, my ichor dripping out of me at an alarming rate, and my mind is muddled, confused.

When a shadow moves at my side, I raise my sword, ready to fight.

But Ladron steps out of the darkness and my breath leaves me in one great exhale as I choke back my emotions.

He takes my hand, his eyes full of worry and tenderness.

"I will slow them down, *Lilyitsa*," he says. "They will think twice before fighting Hermes."

"Come with me," I say, tugging at his hand. "If you stay, Clay will imprison you. Or worse."

He pulls away, his face stoic. "Perhaps it is what we deserve."

"What? What are you talking about?"

"Not everything Clay said was a lie. Before you came to this world, Torak, Mirk and I did conspire to overthrow our fathers. We were tired of their capricious rules. Their outdated ways of governing. We worked with Epimetheus and Apollo to prepare a coup. But when we discovered their plan—that they were to break open the Dungeons, that they were to use fear and chaos to rule—we backed out." He bows his head in shame. "But I realize now, it was too late. I stole the arrows of plague and pestilence from the vaults to return them to Apollo. They had been locked away because of how poisonous they were to the gods."

I'm stunned. "I… this is what you were arguing about when I met you, wasn't it? This is what you and Torak were whispering about?"

"Yes," he admits. "Torak wanted to come clean. But Mirk and I, we wanted to keep our involvement a secret. We were wrong. I am…sorry."

"I—

A pained howl cuts through the night.

Guards rush out of the palace with Clay leading the charge. "There they are. Take them."

"Here," says Ladron, reaching into his cloak to pull out a map. The very one I've been making of the Dungeons. He must have grabbed it once he realized I had to flee. He hands it to me.

"I truly am sorry," says Ladron. And before I can respond, he turns, sword drawn, and charges the guards.

With all my being, I still wish to stay, to fight with him, but I know there will be no victory here.

Prometheus is a Titan. A god older than Zeus himself. He will know what to do.

He is our only hope.

To save my queendom, my men and all those I

have come to care for in this strange new world, I do the hardest thing that has been asked of me so far.

I turn my back on them and flee.

Straight to the cliffs, where the breach is.

And I enter my Dungeons.

"HE IS a man of courage who does not run away, but remains at his post and fights against the enemy."
~*Socrates*

I LEAN AGAINST THE DUNGEON WALL, TRYING TO catch my breath as my wounds begin to reseal themselves. It's all so much to process. Ladron, Mirk, and Torak. Their furtive glances and unfinished sentences make so much sense now. Why they were so willing to be unquestionably tied down to me, to travel with me, to help fix the leaks to the Dungeons.

My emotions are mixed. Part of me feels hurt, used almost, and a little bit angry, but the rest of me understands. Things do need to change in this world. The old ways are outdated.

But there must be a better plan than poisoning the gods in power.

I just hope Prometheus has the answer.

I grab one of Hailey's lamps, which I had left at the breach for my next expedition, and light it with some flint. I don't worry about Clay or his warriors following me here. They will never brave the Dungeons.

I consult my map, studying the paths I have already discovered, particularly the ones I marked as safe. The ones that don't seem to be filled with monsters. There are so many levels now, yet a lot still unmapped, though there's no way of knowing how much I have yet to explore.

After committing my course to memory, I roll the map up, slip it through my belt, and draw my sword.

The air grows cooler the deeper I descend. I keep going down, counting off the passageways one by one, hoping I don't run into anything too deadly, but it's when I hear the dripping of water that I come to an abrupt halt.

I've never heard water before. And it hasn't been raining.

I frown and hold up the lamp.

It's hard to tell exactly where I am, so many of the long passages look the same, filled with nothing more than shadows, cobwebs, and bones, but something glistens on the rock wall to my left. When I get closer, I see rows of crystals embedded in the granite.

"Shit," I mutter under my breath.

I've never been here before.

I turn around to retrace my steps, but within thirty feet, I stumble into a cavern I don't recognize. It's the largest yet, with a massive column rising in the center to support a roof above. And even with Hailey's lamp, there are shadows here large enough to hide who knows what kind of monsters in them.

Soft pings of water drip from the stalactites, but there's another sound just beneath.

I hold my breath and listen.

Breathing. Heavy breathing, and it's close. The hair rises on the back of my neck as goosebumps line my arms.

I'm not alone and whatever it is, from the sound of those lungs, it's big. And obviously, with the brightness of Hailey's lamp reflecting over the cavern, this thing knows I'm here.

"Who is it?" a voice calls out from the shadows on my left.

I jerk, holding the lamp high.

Something bright glints on the cavern floor. A spear. And not just any spear. Mine. The Spear of Truth. The last time I saw it, it was gallivanting across the countryside embedded in the cyclops' eye.

"Who's there?" the voice challenges again.

I grip my sword as I squint at the shadows. Furry legs.

It's the cyclops.

Yet even as I draw myself up, prepared for battle, the creature eases out of the shadows and steps into the light. There's something about the way he moves that gives me pause. It's like he's timid. Cautious. He's nothing like the enraged beast I fought on Mount Olympus.

"Hello?" he prods almost politely, adjusting a large rag that covers most of his eye. The flesh is scarred beneath. He is blind, I realize.

"Hello," I reply, puzzled but wary, ready to attack.

"And to what do I owe the pleasure of your company?" the creature asks, tilting his head in greeting.

Did he really just say that? "I'm… just a traveler. I'm… looking for someone," I say.

"If you tell me who, I would be delighted to be of service," he says with a bow.

I stare, surprised. He's such a gentleman. "Forgive me, but I'm…" I let my voice trail away. Instinct tells me I can trust him, but can I trust my instinct? It seems crazy. Why do I feel like I'm suddenly talking to a long, lost friend?

"Surprised at how civil I am?" he finishes my sentence.

I give an uneasy laugh. "Truthfully, yes. The last cyclops I met was quite…different." And then some. Now, he seems more like the kind who drinks tea and chats about the meaning of ancient poetry.

The cyclops clears his throat and hangs his head. "Ah, that was me," he confesses shyly. "When they dragged me from my home here and gave me that drink, I lost my mind. I wasn't myself. I swear it upon my beloved mother's soul."

Looking at the difference, I can well believe him. "They?" I ask.

"The god that looks like the sun," he offers. "The one that captured the hellhounds."

I hold still. The hellhounds? The god who looks like the sun?

Does he mean Apollo?

I hadn't met him yet, but Ladron mentioned him. It was his arrows that poisoned everyone at the feast.

"Apollo sent the hellhounds?" I ask. "Why?"

I don't really expect an answer, but then, the cyclops says, "That god has been angry ever since the manticore killed the one whose wife opened that box. He sent the hellhounds to fetch him back."

Box? He must be speaking of Pandora's Box and her husband... Epimetheus. Clay. Again. Clay. Apollo and Clay. They were in this together.

Of course.

Ladron, Torak, Mirk, Epimetheus, and Apollo were planning the coup.

My three men backed out, and then Epimetheus must have died. Apollo must have sent the hellhounds to reincarnate his friend early. I was never part of the plan. If Clay had never pushed me, I wouldn't have died that night.

Some things still puzzle me though. I'm unclear on the timeline of events. Heck, I'm unclear if time even moves at the same rate here as it does on earth. But one thing seems certain. Apollo is the mastermind behind all this. Before this is over, I will have to face him. I will have to make him answer for his crimes.

"I need to find Prometheus," I say. "I need his help. Apollo and Clay are up to something very bad."

"Prometheus?" the cyclops asks, his face breaking into a wide smile. "My friend, Prometheus?"

Hope rushes through me. "You know where he is?"

"Of course." The cyclops is practically grinning. "He's not far. Let me show you the way." He takes three steps and then holds up a hand. "Just a minute. I almost forgot." I watch as he backtracks and fumbles on the cavern floor for the spear. "This is yours, I think," he says, handing it to me with a nod.

"I'm sorry," I say, and the words feel so inadequate. "I didn't know you had been drugged."

The cyclops shrugs. "You were protecting the innocent. I would expect nothing less. There are no hard feelings," he says, then sniffs the air. "And no need for weapons. You can sheathe your sword."

He is so aware of everything. I wonder… "Can you still see?" I ask, studying the bandaged eye I threw my spear into what feels like a lifetime ago.

He shakes his head. "No. But I can smell and hear very well."

Guilt claws at me, but then I remember the dismembered bodies, the death and the carnage, and I know I had no choice.

He gestures for me to follow him towards a large doorway. "You're among friends here."

"Friends?" I repeat. "You might be, but there are monsters here. The manticore was hardly the kind I'd call a friend. Not with that venom spike he shot my way."

The cyclops gives me a thoughtful smile. "He's filled with anger. His kind was nearly hunted to extinction. You see, Prometheus didn't just create the Dungeons to protect the world above. He built them to also protect us. Our kind. The victims of so many quests of valor. These Dungeons..." He pauses to spread his hands wide. "This place is a sanctuary. Come, please let me show you."

He leads me through the door and down stone spiral steps. They're worn smooth by the passage of many feet over what must have been many, many years. And the further we descend, the more levels I see, but some of these are lit by creatures that glow in the dark, creatures who stare back at me with cautious, solemn eyes.

There are signs of life everywhere I look, and I know he's right. It's a community, a haven of peace.

How could we all get it so wrong?

"But if it's a sanctuary, why do monsters keep escaping?" I ask. "The manticore? The hydra?"

The cyclops shakes his head. "Not all of us are

pleased to be trapped in such a manner. Some of us miss the fields. The mountains. And some still hate the gods for how they hunted us. They still want revenge."

"And what do you want?" I ask.

The mighty creature sighs, its breath a mist in the air. "I wish for all to dwell in peace. But I fear I will not live to see the day."

We stop walking, and I realize we are standing in front of a stone door with a silver latch. "Here," he says simply.

My heart begins to pound. Prometheus. Finally.

My fingers shake as I lift the latch and cautiously push it open a few inches, clearing my throat to coarsely whisper, "Excuse me? Prometheus?"

When I'm greeted by silence, I push open the door entirely and hold my lantern high.

It's a nice room. Cozy. Just the kind I like. The walls are lined with shelves of scrolls and books. On one side is a bed, covered with a patchworked quilt while drowning in pillows. Who knew Prometheus was a pillow fan just like me? And on the opposite side of the room, there's a polished wooden table covered with books, beeswax candles and—

A skeleton.

It lies by an old fire pit, still bearing a ring and an amulet.

It is all that remains of Prometheus.

"He's dead," I gasp and fall to my knees. "How am I supposed to repair the Dungeons without him? How am I supposed to challenge Clay and Apollo? How am I supposed to save my people? To save Ladron, Torak, and Mirk?"

The old skeleton has no response.

Tears burn my eyes. Clay is going to win. Again. He's a cheater, but that doesn't seem to make a difference. He's still winning. Every. Single. Time.

Gradually, I become aware of a hand—no, a giant finger, patting me awkwardly on the shoulder. The cyclops. He's been nothing but kind from the moment I met him here. He, too, is a victim of Clay and his cronies.

"I'm sorry," I say, my throat closing. "I didn't mean to hurt you. I was just trying to protect—"

"Hush, my friend," the cyclops interrupts me softly.

There's something about the way he says 'friend' that warms my soul. And feels so right. Like I've heard him say it a hundred times before. No… thousands.

Slowly, I lift my head.

The cyclops smiles and nods. "I know who you are. I smelled your scent the moment your spear injured my eye. You're not who you believe yourself to be." He lifts me to my feet. "Hope is not lost, old friend."

Then, the memories begin to return. The many nights we sat together, just him and I, discussing the translations of Aesus over tea and buttered bread. The many creatures we saved. How he, Homer the Brave, helped them adjust to their new lives and gained their trust to find the locations of many more of their kind.

I look down at the spear in my hands, the sword sheathed by my side, and the whip hanging from my belt, and smile. Small wonder I knew how to use these weapons.

"You're right, Homer," I say, giving the cyclops a wry smile. "All hope is not lost. I know what we need to do."

Homer's laugh rings through the room as he bows deep. "Welcome home, Prometheus."

CONTINUE THE ADVENTURE WITH BOOK 2: Warrior Queen on Amazon.

If you enjoyed this book, please consider leaving a review. It helps more than you know!

Want more RH fantasy romance? Check out The Night Firm on Amazon for a complete trilogy.

And don't forget to sign up for our newsletter to never miss a launch on ReadKK.com.

ABOUT KARPOV KINRADE

Karpov Kinrade is the pen name for the wife and husband writing duo of USA TODAY bestselling, award-winning authors Lux Karpov-Kinrade and Dmytry Karpov-Kinrade.

Together, they live in Ukiah, California where they write fantasy romance novels and screenplays, make music and direct movies.

Look for more from Karpov Kinrade in *Dungeon Queen, Mad Girl, Bad Witch, The Night Firm, Vampire Girl, Of Dreams and Dragons, Nightfall*

Academy and *Paranormal Spy Academy*. If you're looking for their suspense and contemporary romance titles, you'll find those under Alex Lux.

They live with their three teens who share a genius for all things creative, and seven cats who think they rule the world (spoiler, they do.)

Want their books and music before anyone else and also enjoy weekly interactive flash fiction? Join them on Patreon at Patreon.com/karpovkinrade

Find them online at KarpovKinrade.com

On Facebook /KarpovKinrade

On Twitter @KarpovKinrade

And subscribe to their newsletter at ReadKK.com for special deals and up-to-date notice of new launches.

~ ~ ~ ~ ~

If you enjoyed this book, consider supporting the author by leaving a review wherever you purchased this book. Thank you.

ABOUT LIV CHATHAM

For Liv Chatham, one life is not enough, but she solved that problem by living vicariously through her characters in fantastic worlds. When she's not reading, she's biking to the nearest coffee shop to cuddle with a latte and write, and then she's biking back home again to cuddle with her French Bulldog and write some more.

Since she doesn't like to hold still, she doesn't stay long in one place, and because she's naturally nosy, she's lived and travelled in over forty countries around the world. By nature, she's a fantasy and paranormal addict, but since she's never met a word she didn't like, she'll dabble in other genres from time to time.

Sign up for Liv's newsletter at http://www.LivChatham.com and become her friend at Facebook: https://www.facebook.com/author.liv.chatham

Dungeon Queen

Warrior Queen

By Karpov Kinrade & Liv Chatham

A fantasy romance reverse harem with greek mythology and badassery.

The Winter Witch

by Karpov Kinrade & Heather Hildenbrand

A standalone fairytale fantasy romance retelling with magic and wonder.

Mad Girl: Locked Up

Mad Girl: Fights Back

by Karpov Kinrade & Heather Hildenbrand

A paranormal reverse harem romance with magic, mystery and madness.

The Night Firm

I Am the Wild

I Am the Storm

I Am the Night

A fantasy reverse harem romance with mystery and depth.

Wanted by Karpov Kinrade & Liv Chatham

A standalone dark paranormal romance that's a spin off of The Night Firm.

In the Vampire Girl Universe

A fantasy romance series with mystery and magic.

Vampire Girl

Vampire Girl 2: Midnight Star

Vampire Girl 3: Silver Flame

Vampire Girl 4: Moonlight Prince

Vampire Girl 5: First Hunter

Vampire Girl 6: Unseen Lord

Vampire Girl 7: Fallen Star

Vampire Girl: Copper Snare

Vampire Girl: Crimson Cocktail

Vampire Girl: Christmas Cognac

Of Dreams and Dragons

Get the soundtrack for I AM THE WILD, OF DREAMS AND DRAGONS and MOONSTONE ACADEMY wherever music can be found.

Nightfall Academy

A fantasy dystopian academy series with double lives, intrigue and romance.

Court of Nightfall

Weeper of Blood

House of Ravens

Night of Nyx

Song of Kai

Daughter of Strife

Paranormal Spy Academy (complete academy sci fi thriller romance)

A paranormal romance with mystery and superpowers.

Forbidden Mind

Forbidden Fire

Forbidden Life

Our ALEX LUX BOOKS!

The Seduced Saga (paranormal romance with suspense)

Seduced by Innocence

Seduced by Pain

Seduced by Power

Seduced by Lies

Seduced by Darkness

The Call Me Cat Trilogy (romantic suspense)

Call Me Cat

Leave Me Love

Tell Me True

(Standalone romcon with crossover characters)

Hitched

Whipped

Kiss Me in Paris (A standalone romance)

Our Children's Fantasy collection under Kimberly Kinrade

The Three Lost Kids series

Lexie World

Bella World

Maddie World

The Three Lost Kids and Cupid's Capture

The Three Lost Kids and the Death of the Sugar Fairy

The Three Lost Kids and the Christmas Curse